Bottle Talk

Bottle Talk

Short Short Fiction

Ken Rivard

Black Moss Press
2002

Published by Black Moss Press at 2450 Byng Road, Windsor, Ontario N8W 3E8. Black Moss books are distributed in Canada and the U.S. by Firefly Books, 3680 Victoria Park Ave., Willowdale, Ont. Canada. All orders should be directed there.

Black Moss would like to acknowledge the generous support of the Canada Council and the Ontario Arts Council for its publishing program.

The Canada Council | Le Conseil des Arts
for the Arts | du Canada

ONTARIO ARTS COUNCIL
CONSEIL DES ARTS DE L'ONTARIO

National Library of Canada Cataloguing in Publication
Rivard, Ken, 1947-
        Bottle talk / Ken Rivard.

ISBN 0-88753-371-X

        I. Title.

PS8585.I8763B68 2002   C813'.54   C2002-
903041-2
PR9199.3.R5256B68 2002

Acknowledgements

Portions of this book have appeared in *Other Voices* and *The Prairie Journal of Canadian Literature*.

This book is dedicated to H.P. and to Michilene,

Other Books By Ken Rivard

Kiss Me Down To Size (Poetry,1983).

Frankie's Desires (Poetry,1987).

If She Could Take All These Men (Postcard or short, short fiction,1995) - Finalist for The Writers Guild Of Alberta, Howard O'Hagan, 1996 Best Short Fiction Book Award.

Mom, The School Flooded (Children's Book,1996).

Skin Tests (Postcard or short, short fiction, 2000) - Finalist for The Writers Guild Of Alberta, Howard O'Hagan, 2001, Best Short Fiction Book Award and Finalist for The City of Calgary, 2001, W.O. Mitchell Book Prize.

Boyfriend

"Not a word. Not a sound.

My mother's secret boyfriend pays us to keep quiet. And Dad never knows what's going on. Me and my brother and sister go over to the boyfriend's with my mom. He takes out a huge jar of change. Pennies. Nickles. Dimes. Quarters. Piles of coins on the coffee-table. And the boyfriend tells us to carefully count everything. All we count, we keep. He starts our counting by presenting to each of us, a fistful of pennies that look like they come from a second jar we never see. We call it The Nowhere Jar. While we count, my mom and her boyfriend disappear into his bedroom. We know. We turn up the radio. Force ourselves to listen to songs we love. Songs we don't know. Songs we hate.

My dad's a really good man. I say he's like the lemon-yellow warmth of the sun. Mom says he's a lemon. He has to work the nightshift all the time. Don't think he ever knows about Mom and her secret boyfriend. I wonder what he and his lemon-yellow warmth would do.

Anyhow, my brother and sister and me make a pile of money every time we go to the secret boyfriend's place. We don't feel exactly right but the money sure comes in handy. And for about a year my father can't figure out where we get the extra toys. What really gets my dad are the new clothes we sometimes wear to school. He must know he didn't pay for them. Then the boyfriend starts using bigger and bigger jars with more and more pennies. Too many pennies. Too many. Makes holes. Lots of holes. In our pockets.

One night I start counting the copper lies in my sleep and I wish they'd jingle, like coins do, but they don't. They are bigger than plates, bigger than manhole covers. And The Nowhere Jar is the size of my bedroom.

Not a word. Not a sound."

Three Times She's A Lady

"I only do it three times a year but I still need help for my boozing.

What I did was buy a case of champagne and drink every last drop by myself. I booked off work for a few days. Told the boss I'm in the hospital and not allowed to have visitors. Three times a year. Once in the Fall. Once in the Winter. Once in the Spring. I usually made it through the summer dry. I'm an excellent employee. A top professional on the job. A real lady too. The boss never questioned me about my hospital visits. And the champagne made the fear go away. I could be whoever I wanted to be for a week or so and felt wonderfully scared. During my last binge, I became someone I thought I'd never be. No control at all. Stumbled along The Left Bank in Paris. Nearly choked on the neck of a bottle and rolled into The Seine River. Woke up in a somewhere bed. Woke up with a man I'd never recommend , even to my ex-mother-in-law. The first sip killed me. Yes, that first sip sent me places three times a year. My sponsor says I broke out in spots like Montreal, New York or Paris, where I pretended in another language. Be a bilingual drunk. Learned to throw up in French.

Whenever I looked at my glass, it was neither half-full or half-empty. Only too small. Even for champagne. In public though, I stuck with those long, thin-stemmed glasses you hold between your third and fourth fingers, the ones that felt like my bones did after a binge. I was born thirsty."

Dogs And The Bathroom

"I love to drive my Cocker Spaniel nuts whenever I get a buzz on. It takes me about three to four beer. My dog follows me into the bathroom when I go for my first big pee. You know the kind of pee I mean: the one where your insides want to split their way out of you, like angry flowers from the soil or something.

She watches the yellow stream arcing into the toilet bowl. I move further and further from the bowl and then pee into the bathtub or sink. My dog hates this, maybe because she is smart enough to know how to use the bathtub and sink. Yet, she starts running in small circles and I move closer and closer to the bowl. Then I suddenly jump back and make my dog frantic. Anyone watching this would wonder why I am trying to push my dog over the edge. Circles. Circles. Doing the same thing over and over again and expecting different results each time.

Later, after a few more beer, I do it all over again until my dog is making faster and faster circles on the bathroom floor. Makes me laugh as hard as a machine gun listening to the dog howl and howl. Crazy dog. Crazy drunk. I loved my craziness because I was far funnier than when I was between drunks.

Even after being dry all these years, I still laugh whenever I go for a sober pee, whenever I remember that I cannot drink just for today or those circles will strangle me.

You know the kind of pee I mean."

Creative Talking

"I'm invited to give a talk on creativity to a bunch of school-teachers who work with gifted kids. My host treats me to a breakfast fit for an emperor. We talk about the way ideas take shape. I impress her with the 'what if's' of imagining. I know that by the way both her eyes and smile grow in size and the way she brings her hand to her mouth while dropping her head and sliding her legs together. She takes my phone number to call sometime about her own poems and stories. I wouldn't mind impressing her lots more. Away from here.

I give my talk. The teachers say I spoke like a guy with a big city accent. They say they learned a lot about jumping off their pretending. Good. That is exactly what I wanted but hadn't really planned for. Creativity. Funny how it works on one side of the brain.

After my presentation, the host takes me upstairs to a hospitality room where free booze can be had. Two big forty ouncers of rye sit on the table right in front of me. Hello, the bottles say to me. Hello. I pour myself a stiff one with a shot or two of ginger ale. Down the hatch. Then a second drink. Stiffer. Suddenly, my host tells me I'm not the same person she's been with all day, that I've become a stranger from the streets. She's right. It's like I've changed faces since that first sip and my first face doesn't even know it. The woman leaves. Says she's sorry she ever asked for my phone number. And soon everyone else around the table of my brilliance has left too because I'm just too sensitive, too inventive with my muttering because… I am always on my mind."

Rye And The Sink

"I'm at my buddy's house to put away a mickey of rye before heading to the party. We are soon halfway in the bag and then weave our way over to the party. After one or two beer, I have to get to the can in the rumpus room. My stomach keeps pushing its way up my throat and wants to leave me. I grab onto the sink and I feel my insides coming up from my toes. But nothing happens. I just tremble so much my clothes nearly fall off. I grab onto the sink again and I try to force the vomit out of me. Nothing. Then I grab the sink a third time really hard and I pull it out of the wall and it hangs knee-high, like a huge porcelain ear. Soon there is vomit all over the place. Floor. Walls. Mirror. Bathtub. Shower curtains. Lights. Everywhere but in the sink or toilet. And lots of water too!. Oh! Oh! So I head outside and fall to my knees on the cold, wet grass. Then, I grab onto a steel fence separating this backyard from the one next door and puke at the moon. Soon, three men from the party come outside. They are friends of the host. They want to know why I yanked the sink from the wall.Unbelievably, my drunk friend comes outside and begs them to leave me there hanging onto the fence. He tells them I've been sick for days and that they could easily kill me with one kick or punch. They are told that I'll call tomorrow and pay for the sink. The men nod, then vanish. My friend takes off too, probably back to the party. I look at my bloodied knuckles. Wipe my face. See my pain written in the stars. Give the moon another dose of its own medicine.

Who will clean up this black sink of sky after I'm done?"

More Than Your's

"After I leave this D.D. meeting, I'm going home to blow my wife's head off. I've had enough of her. What's that? You think if I hang around here, I feel better. Ha! I doubt it. If some women didn't have a vagina, there'd be a bounty on their heads. I know. I know. I'm lucky this is a closed men's meeting. Bet women sometimes say the same thing about men. Ya. Ya. Ya. I know. I know. Politically correct. I should just listen. Right?

Now that the meeting's over, I feel more serene but my wife still has to go. She's getting in the way of me staying sober and I'll do anything to keep my sobriety. What's that you say? You want me to shoot your wife too because she's a pain in the ass. And you want me to take you out to my truck and show you my gun? What? You want us to go to your place right now and kill your wife first. Might as well do two for the price of one. Now? Right now? You're crazy. Nuts. Okay. Okay. You're right. I'm the one who's insane. Maybe, I've been missing too many of my anger management courses or perhaps I'm like that guy who keeps walking in front of a moving bus and almost getting killed each time but still continues doing it expecting something amazing to happen every time. What makes it scarier is that I'd probably make sure it was the same bus number every time.

Three days ago my wife told me that my gerbil's dead but the wheel is still spinning, spinning.

My gun is still cocked."

Hit And Run

"Just knocked over a convenience store when I thought I should head to a D.D. meeting for some quick serenity and a spiritual tuneup before skipping town. Should have seen the scared look on that clerk's face. Think he wet his pants. Lost his accent, then his voice too. He even offered me a free coffee. Sorry if I'm late. Looks like the meeting is almost over. I have time for a very quick coffee and an even quicker prayer. What's in my plastic, 7-Eleven bag? Yep. That's right. My loot. Here's a fistful of bills for the collection basket. I'll stay for a few minutes or so. Do some sharing. Listen. Whoops, I hear sirens. Gotta go boys. Still haven't had a drink today but for the grace of God. One day at a time. Oh, and by the way, thanks for the coffee. Take extra time to go out to your vehicles, guys. Could be cops everywhere. Might slow you down on the way home. If people ask if you've seen a guy who looks like me, tell them 'no'. No is the safest place for me right now. If you're forced to, tell them I've left for No. What's that? First things first? Sure. Sure."

I Need Help

"It's about four-thirty in the morning and I'm driving home to my wife after being out on a real beer spree with a buddy. I'm two minutes away from home when I drive right through a red light on a busy boulevard. You know. Montreal. Never goes to bed. Always alive. Even at four in the morning. Anyhow, this driver coming the other way stops just in time. I pull over just past the intersection. I look back at the driver driving slowly across the intersection. Hope he doesn't get hit. But he knows. His sad look and shaking head tell I could have been killed. One second his face is whiter than flour and the next, redder than a mother's blood after childbirth. Must be my Greater Spirit keeping an eye on me or something. I drive the rest of the way home in a cold, cold sweat. Stunned sober. The sun wants to come up like the bottom of my stomach does. I know my wife will be furious. And she is. She says she almost left me for a motel room. Where the hell was I? Her words are knives. I tell my wife I was out drinking. Too close to the killing. Too close. I need help. I'm cut from the inside out. Sliced scared. Too scared to be in my skin anymore.

She picks up the phone."

The Next Day Corpse

"I love my organ and piano music. Keeps me alive for hours. I also love my gin. Funerals. I play lots of them. When I wake up the next day with the usual hangover, I go to work in some church somewhere. There's something about the insides of a church that makes my stomach churn. The smells. Candle wax. Incense. Wooden pews. Stuffy leftover smells. Stale as the insides of my shoes. I'm probably a recovering Catholic too. So so many Catholics in D.D. It's not God's fault. And I always sit down with my butt polishing the piano bench, swishing back and forth, as if I want my real face to show. But looking at the corpse in the coffin not far from the organ, makes me push the vomit back inside of me, as if I own two stomachs, as if only dead bodies cause stomach indigestion. I'd love to tell the dead body to move over and make room for me, there in the quiet satin. But I just play. Play my music. Sing a holy gin song.

Did I tell you that I took out a second mortgage on my house to get money to record my first C.D.? Did I also tell you that my husband died in his wheelchair from self-pity? Did I tell you that my organ is my heart?

I just play my music and sing myself holy."

Whiskey Dog

"Life is a joke and my dog is the punch line.

I stumble home drunker than any skunk could possibly be and stagger into my dark kitchen. Nobody greets me. Imagine that. Nobody but my dog. My hunting dog. The rest of the family shuts me out from behind their bedroom doors. Only my dog loves me and I appreciate him. So, I give him a bowl of whiskey and fresh cream. The dog laps it all up but soon has difficulty making it either up or down the stairs to go outside for a pee.

The next night the same thing happens and I offer my dog another bowl of whiskey and fresh cream. No matter how hard I try, the dog refuses to drink from his saucer. I try pushing my dog's head into the saucer. I try holding the saucer up to his face. Nothing. I even try pouring some dried dog food on top of the whiskey and cream. Nothing. Finally, my dog growls and nips at my fingers, as if he owns the good part of my half-wittedness. Nobody greets me."

That Moment

"I wish it would be compulsory for her to listen whenever she opens her mouth.

I really hate that moment right after we finish supper. You know the one – when it's so quiet you can almost hear the leftovers cooling off. And I cringe because I know my wife is going to bring it up again. She's going to make a long, loud list of all my defects of character – especially the ones that have anything to do with keeping her happy. My selfishness. My self-centeredness. The ones that made me drink when I did. The ones I still have. I know. I know. She's right. But now I am sober and it's as if she wants to turn me inside out, so she could dryclean me every night after feeding me and then drape plastic over me like one of those living room sofas that nobody ever sits on. Now, I just turn her off. Smile. Nod. Smile. Nod again. Knot my forehead. Cringe. Look concerned. Other times I have to slip away from the supper table as fast as possible because I know how my wife must fill that moment. Usually, I head to the bathroom, close the door, lock it, get on my knees and pray over and over. I keep the bathroom light off because the darkness gives me more power there on the hard marble floor. Why? I don't know.

I wish. I wish."

Baby Bottle

"Hey you, stop that whining, will ya. Here take this baby bottle. Stuff it in your mouth. Yea, pity pot. Your pity pot. Now, each of you grab onto your own imaginary baby bottle and let's toast that whiner over there. Yea, you! Don't worry. We're not laughing at you but with you! So you lost your job and you owe money. Your wife has left you. So? So? Hey, what are you doing? No, I don't want to go ten rounds with you outside. Just want to keep you sober. Getting off the booze is only a part of it. Now, ya gotta learn to live. Forget all the stuff your parents and school taught you. Forget everything you learned in books, especially psychology books. And we're all here for you. Remember we're laughing with you, not at you. That means we've all had the same feelings. Got it? Now, listen to the laughing will ya! Get to know the difference. And then… then, stop your whining!"

Jump

"I just wanna die. One day I'm gonna commit suicide. You'll see. You'll see.

What's that you say? Do I really want to die? Do it, you say. Do it. You want me to come with you. You'll drive me to die? Okay. Okay. I'll come with you. I'll show you! Let's go. Where's your vehicle? Okay, let's go. Put on your seat belt. Roll down your window. You'll see. You'll see. Don't believe me, eh?

Hey, what are we doing on this bridge? Why are we stopped here? Get out? You want me to get out and jump? Right now? Wait. Wait. Stop pushing me. What do you mean by "have a good jump?" You're kidding. All right. I'll do it. What's that? You don't think I have the guts to do it, eh! Well, watch. Just watch me. Hey, what are you doing? You're pushing me. Helping me climb up on the railing. Are you nuts? I'm not jumping off this bridge! What's that? Yea. Yea, I promise not to talk about it anymore at the Don't Drink meetings. And I'll only die when I learn how not to be afraid of death. Okay. Got it. I think. "

Grade Eight Intellect

"My mother was a hairdresser and she brought me up all by herself. Had my own bedroom in the back of her salon. I love women. I keep falling in love with them, all because of that room in the hairdressing salon. My shrink, who is a woman herself, said it may have something to do with hearing so many women voices so often.

I went as far as Grade Eight in school and then joined the navy. Took me years to find out what the difference was between being educated and intelligent. Anytime I meet anyone with more education than me, I tell them that they are educated beyond their intellects – even before they open their mouths because... I know. I'm self-educated. Travelled the world in the navy. My own university. My mother's backroom. Where's my intellect now? Certainly not back in Grade Eight. And women think I'm brilliant. All this, thanks to my mother. Not school. And not you or your voice spray of higher learning."

Aqua Velva And The Fried Egg

"Me and another recovering drunk are out at a flophouse- rooming-house downtown. The place looks like it could all collapse at any time, like a rotting house of cards. We go up the stairs and they creak, as if we are in a scary movie. You know the ones. Then we knock on the door. A naked man of about fifty-five stands there holding a half-empty bottle of Aqua Velva After-Shave Lotion. His face is a poorly gravelled road. We tell him we're here because he called for help.

On the man's floor is an uncovered mattress. A hot-plate over in the corner is red-hot with an upside-down Kraft Peanut Butter tin jar lid on top. In the lid, is a partially fried egg, sizzling, sizzling. The man tells us he's starving and doesn't want to die, his breath sweet with the smell of shaving lotion.

We dress him. I finish frying his egg. He eats with a large spoon from the peanut butter jar lid, holding the lid with his sock so it doesn't burn his fingers. Let him slurp a last sip of after-shave. Pour the rest in the toilet at the end of the hall. Take him downstairs for coffee. Talk until one a.m.. Bring him back upstairs. Check for more bottles of Aqua Velva. Put him to bed. Promise we'll be back at eight a.m. to take him for breakfast and then a detox center. Go home scared but confident.

We return the next morning. Take him for bacon and eggs. He eats two breakfasts. Four eggs. Ten strips of bacon. Eight pieces of toast. And coffee. Lots of coffee. After we drive him to the detox center but they have no room. So we take him back to my friend's rumpus room where he drinks the place dry of all soft drinks. Then, finally, we get a phone call from the detox. They'll take him in one hour.

Tonight, I'll still be talking to him in my sleep."

Ink

"Where did I get all these tattoos? From all over the world. Women, all of them real beauties! All of them made my toes curl. Here's Christina from Barcelona. Mary Lou from New Jersey. Betty from New York City. Olivia from Calgary. Monique from Montreal. Women. Ink. Stories on my forearms. Movies on my biceps. Novels on my chest. Bestsellers, all of them. And you should see the rest of me. They're with me forever, these ink loves.

What's that you say? I don't need more coffee? Just a cup of ink. Watch it! I'm an ex-army man. You'll be wearing my fist up your nose. I know. I know. You're laughing with me, not at me. Did I ever show you the tattoo on the palm of my right hand? Take a close look. See that? It's an airplane tattoo. Got it on Yonge Street in Toronto. I once flew from Toronto to Amsterdam all because I went to Pearson Airport for a few drinks. All on a dare. My buddy made me do it. Gotta blame someone. Anyhow, before I know it, I'm landing in Amsterdam at eight a.m., Amsterdam time. No suitcase. No money. Just my credit card and for some reason or other, my passport. And my airplane tattoo with the ink barely dry. I'm roaring drunk, shoving, stumbling through the airport crowd, yelling at anyone in my way. Then, one guy offers me a swig from his flask of whiskey. I grab the flask with my tattooed hand and promise that I'll fly anywhere he wants."

Accountants And Hookers

"Not bad for an old geezer.

That's right. It's my belly button birthday today. Sixty years old. Not bad for an old geezer. But my Don't Drink birthday is much more important. I celebrated that one last month. Twenty years sober. Should have seen what my home group gave me for a gift. A hooker. That's right, the group bought a hooker and the guy who won her in a draw, went with her after me. I couldn't believe it. I thought it was all a joke. And I'd been working hard at getting away from seeing women as sex objects. Sure enough, at the end of the meeting, a very well-dressed woman, in a dark blue suit of all things, walked into our meeting and gently took me by the hand. She looked more like an accountant than a hooker. She even carried a briefcase that made her look like she was going to do my books. Well, she brought me up to her apartment just a few blocks away. Didn't take me long to find out she wasn't an accountant at all. Nosiree. Felt as good or as bad as my last drunk before I joined Don't Drink. Depends how you look at it. Know what I mean? Good thing my home group is a closed men's group, though. Good thing another guy had her after me.

Not bad for an old geezer."

Crop Duster

"Been a part-time farmer and part-time crop duster with my small plane. Used to drink my face off until midnight at the latest. Seems like my last drunk was when I lost my face forever. Think I puked it up to the stars. Don't know how I did it but I was always awake at five a.m., getting ready to board my small airplane and get out there to dust crops. I'd climb into the cockpit and fly off into the sunrise. Always wondered if I ever killed anyone but I never drank past midnight, just to be sure. I'd have a hangover as big as the sky and sometimes it felt like I was flying into a roaring furnace. My aim seemed to be pretty good with that dust. Never had any complaints from the farmers. Always felt as if I was surrounded by two motors: one being the actual engine of the aircraft and the other, that hangover noise between my ears. Both motors got louder and louder and I had to join Don't Drink. Now, there is only one motor running and it asks me killer questions in sobriety such as why was I always pushing my feelings back down into my stomach, like I tried to do with my vomit on so many occasions. Or did I ever kill anyone with my airplane? Everyone says that, despite myself, if I keep coming back to D.D. meetings, I'll get the answers I need, not the ones I want. And I'd really like my face back too."

Holes

"I work as an auto body man and I should know better.   Just finished punching more holes in my bedroom walls. My new wife keeps buying more cheap mirrors and pictures to cover the holes. You should see our bedroom! Looks like a cross between a movie star's makeup room and a museum.

Next day, I'm in a treatment centre having everything, including my fist, repaired. Good thing I go there. For the first day or so, they put me in a rubber room where all the punching in the world isn't going to make any difference. I drink coffee, caffeine-free, with no cream or sugar. So so black. Like the holes in the vehicles I fix or the holes in my bedroom walls.

When I get out of treatment, I stop at the hardware store and get everything I need to fix my bedroom walls. My intentions are good, if not great.

At home, my wife welcomes me back and takes me up to our bedroom. I'm thinking… wow, she's really, really glad to see me. But as soon as I open the bedroom door, I see our walls covered with posters, cheap pictures and mirrors. She asks me to look into each and every mirror. Then she removes each after I've had a look. She doesn't look or sound too glad to see me. I'm thinking sex and she's got wall fixing on her mind. When I say that WE should patch up all the holes, she tells me that I have to do it. Not her. And I work through the entire night patching up each and every hole while my wife sleeps on the couch downstairs.

By morning, I am finished and she finally shows me how glad she is I'm home.

I work as an auto body man and I should know better."

Initials

"I am sixty-three years old and people in D.D. say my speech sounds like the very finest sandpaper.

I've been sober for a long time and I once heard someone say my bleached blonde hair has been colored so often that it has become straw left out in the sun forever. Actually, I hate the sun; it reminds me of a huge silent scream, the kind of scream I heard in my sleep towards the end of my drinking. And when you're talking to your Greater Spirit, and asking for something, He'll usually tell you: yes, no, or wait.

Last week I was in my husband's restaurant having an after-meeting snack with some D.D. members. One of the guys ordered a grilled ham and cheese. When the sandwich arrived there was no ham in it. I told the waitress to take it back but the guy was so hungry, he said he's eat it like it was. I told him he should get what he ordered and the waitress just scooped it off our table. I'm sure he's one of those men who doesn't understand what WAIT means. Anyway, the right sandwich arrived and I checked to make sure the ham was there and it was. But there were two hairs on top of the sandwich that I swore looked like my ex-husband's initials. Bet he was working in the kitchen that night. Wait'll I tell him what

I know.

"Ocean Floating"People look at the tattoo of the Pacific Ocean on my upper arm and often say that I speak as sincerely as a light morning rain. I'm flattered. I've never been honest a day in my life when I was drinking. But my Pacific Ocean is fading and I'm scared. Terrified actually. I gotta meet a drug dealer I used to do business with before I sobered up. I'm supposed to meet him tonight after this D.D. meeting. Said I'd meet him at a Tim Horton's. Lots of lighting there. Need a safe place to tell this dealer that he doesn't have to go after my kid brother's legs to get me to pay back what I owe. I don't have any money right now but I haven't used or drank for nearly thirty days now. Yet, I know I have to make amends and pay this guy back for all the highs the dope gave me, for all the highs I fell from. My D.D. sponsor told me yesterday that it's time to start the D.D. steps, that my ocean floating has got to stop and only then will I really be able to live up to my tattoo."

Da Wife

"As you can see I love eating red licorice when I talk. And I need to have my Big Gulp Coke too. Just me, my licorice, my Coke and… the ceiling.

When I did my inventory step, I thought that was it. I listed all my defects of character. My assets. A list of everything from the time I was a kid. I thought I was as thorough and as honest as possible. Then da wife got a hold of the list by accident. She found it rolled up in one of my shoes. Then she added a lot more defects which she says I may have forgotten about. My list grew and grew, as if da wife gave it new life. She also crossed off some of the assets I thought I had and added others. She said I forgot to mention that I was a man who persevered. Then she added even more defects such as being that hero on a white, white horse who really only saves people in distress so he can tell them that he saved them, they owed him and when will they pay him back. She didn't even bother to place my list back into the same shoe. Just left it there in the middle of my dresser. She's so subtle that way.

After, I asked her why she still wanted to stay married to me and she told me she loved the new sober me, even if I can't stop looking at the ceiling whenever I talk.

So, da wife is a helluva woman. I couldn't ask for more. I wouldn't ask for more. As you can see."

Mustache, Sex And Roy Orbison

"My sister says I have a voice that can calm a mother who has just lost her only child in a raging fire. Sexy voice, she tells me. Just thinking about her words makes me want to stroke my thick mustache and brush it up my cheeks until it tickles my eyes. Ah, sex! Don't you think my mustache looks like two black, horny caterpillars hanging on the edges of my mouth. That's the image I want. Notice my hair. Friends say that it doesn't know which way is up or down and that's just perfect for me. And I always wear black, like Roy Orbison. Black is honest, Roy Orbison honest.

I married for sex only. It was like fraud. A great way to legalize our sex. It was that good! But I can't live like that anymore. Can't lie. Couldn't lie if I tried. Yesterday I was in a Mac's store picking up my Calgary Sun and morning coffee. The clerk gave me twenty cents too much in change. I gave him back his twenty cents right then and there. It's like sex. I have to be straight about it all. Honest. Otherwise, I push my Greater Spirit away. And I could get drunk again.

They say that Roy Orbison lost his first family in a fire and after that he wore black. Bet he didn't marry just for sex. They say his last lover was a mystery girl.

My sister says she knows my voice better than anyone."

Caught Him

"Friends say I look like a James Bond twin and there were times when I believed them, even though I've never worn a tuxedo ever.

One night last week I felt just like a sneaky spy working for the good guys. I was sleeping soundly at home when I heard this rustling noise beside my bed. I opened one eye a little and saw this thief going through my jeans on the floor. In his right hand was one of those pen-sized flashlights. I pretended to still be asleep. As soon as he got close enough and his back was slightly turned, I jumped out of bed and nailed him. I scared him so much that he actually screamed. Then, I pinned him on the floor. Told him I'd stuff his pen flashlight into his eye socket if he made one move. And he didn't budge. Until I called the cops. Then he pushed me off and jumped to his feet. Just as he was taking off, I grabbed my aluminum baseball bat and flung it at the back of his legs. Should have heard him scream as he hit the floor. You should have seen what I did with his pen flashlight. Don't think he'll ever blow his nose the same way again.

When the cops came they asked me if I had ever been arrested for assault and I said I was only trying to stay sober. Would James Bond have been more polite?"

Biking In The Wind

"Got this bald head from all my years of biking to school in the wind. I lived in a city of wind. Wild wind. Overpowering wind. Wind that had no respect for roots. On the way to school, I used to pray to God asking for strength to make it through the wind wall. I talked. I prayed. I talked. I prayed, as if God were a compassionate weatherperson. Used to beg God to tie the wind into knots.

On the way home though, I smiled a lot and didn't pray to anyone for anything. The wind was at my back. Hardly had to pedal. I was carried along with thick, strong, cool hands, like a kite on two wheels, until I reached my front door.

So now, when the wind is in my face, I pray. When it's at my back, there's no need for praying. That is until yesterday when I started doing 'just in case' praying because the wind shifted twice.

And as far as my bald head is concerned, whenever some guy rubs it and says it feels just like his wife's bum, I just touch my high forehead with my fingertips and say that he is absolutely right.

Tomorrow, I will look for more wind."

Bed

"Get those creatures out of my bed! There. On the bedspread. On top of my pillow. Black wings fluttering on white. Don't believe me? Pull the blankets and sheets off. See! Listen, I'm not getting into that bed until you strip everything off. Right now! Okay. Okay. I believe you. The creatures are gone. Go ahead. Make the bed again. Wait. Look! They're back! More creatures than ever before. Strip the bed again. Please! See. They're still there. Pull the mattress off. Now the box-spring. Check the floor. The corners. Okay, put everything back. Move the bed closer to the window. Open the window. Let the creatures out. No! No! Don't do that! Those slimy things will slip in through the cracks around the window. Yea, the cracks. Or they'll just fly through the glass. Bet their wings are that sharp, that strong. Sleep with me! Sleep with me! That'll do it. You'd never act like a creature. Would you? Naw, it's not in you."

Bruises

"See this fading, purple-red welt under my eye? It's a leftover from my late husband. All we did together was drink, fight and have great sex. In bed the fighting just disappeared. As soon as we put on our clothes though, he'd raise his fists and tell me I'm nothing more than a whore.

One day, I came home with a police officer and my husband locked himself in the bathroom with a few bottles of rye. Drink. Drink. Drink. He'd gone over the edge. I'd had enough of my own boozing. He was sure scared when he saw me with that cop. While me and the cop got to know each other better, if you know what I mean. When we finally got the bathroom door open, my hubby was dead, floating in the bathtub with one wrist slashed and his other hand clenched like a fist pointing upwards, as if the skylight were an evil eye that finally got to him and convinced him that my vagina wasn't only his, like his fists are."

Smart Punching

"Used to play pro-hockey in The American Hockey League. I'd go out on the ice and pick scraps with guys who were six inches taller than me and win. Then, after the game, I'd go for a few beer with the same guys I had fought with. Later, I'd go home to my woman. And she'd beat me. No kidding. I'd come to the rink with a black eye, a broken nose and bruises everywhere. The other guys on the team just couldn't figure out why I came to the rink all beat up. I'd make up all kinds of excuses, wild stories about tripping, falling, getting hit by a door, a gate, anything. Then one day my right-winger came over to my place without warning and rang my doorbell. When I opened the door, he took one look at me and told me that I am leaving this abusive relationship. I packed up and left. No note. Nothing for my wife. My buddy drove me all the way over to my parents' place where I stayed until I felt better.

Imagine, I spent a year and a half in an abusive relationship with that woman. I just couldn't hit her back. It was the first real relationship I had with a woman. My first sex. Nobody believed me. Nobody. And I don't get into as many fights on the ice now. I pick my spots and I don't have to pretend anymore."

Talking Through Chicago

"I roll my own. I plan to get into a recovery center soon to get on with the business of getting sober. See this tobacco, these cigarette papers? I bartered for them. I barter for everything. I make a living showing others how to barter.

Last week I went to a convention of barterers in Chicago. I promised I wouldn't drink but I had a couple of rye and ginger ale's. Just two drinks. Then I stopped. Did all kinds of bartering deals on those two drinks. Not a dollar exchanged hands. So what! I had a slip. Yes, I want to get sober. Haven't you ever had a slip and went out drinking again? You haven't? Well goodie goodie for you! You're lucky. You say I have three choices : 1. drink and die, 2. drink and be locked up in a loony bin and 3. not drink and live. Well don't get mad at me because I had ONE slip. What's that? To hell with the bartering? Are you crazy? It's my life. Yes, I want to get off the booze. Yes, I want to live. Not your way though. Don't call me, I'll call you. I'm going back to Chicago. I left something there.

I roll my own."

Bedroom Of Insanity

"What I really want is to have one last drunk. A real dandy! I'll fill up my bedroom with as many booze bottles as it can hold. Then I want you two guys in D.D. to stand guard at my door, one at a time. Don't let me out of my bedroom until I drink every last drop. And don't allow anyone in. That's right. Not a soul. Think of it. You're helping me quit booze. I'll be able to thank you both. I'll be done with the drinking, thanks to your watching over me. And after my last binge, I'll never touch booze again. What do you mean you can't do that? Aren't you from D.D., that Don't Drink group? Aren't you here to help me get sober? Get the hell out of here then! And take your message with you. No! Wait! Wait!"

Saved By An Undertaker

"I work as a carpenter and I've tried everything to stay sober. Psych Wards. Counsellors. Psychologists. Psychiatrists. Priests. Ministers. Family. Friends. Nobody, nothing could stop me from drinking. I tried control drinking. After, I switched from scotch to wine, then to beer and eventually, light beer.

Finally, I called D.D. and told a stranger on the phone that I was beaten, whipped by this baffling booze and that I couldn't stand myself anymore. The voice told me to wait by the phone, that a man would be calling in a few minutes. Shortly afterwards, a guy phoned and after we spoke for just a few minutes, he said he had just come home from work but he'd pick me up shortly to go to a D.D. meeting. An undertaker showed up in his hearse, dressed for work in a black suit, white shirt and black tie. He also had a dead body in the back. He told me if I was going to get sober I had to follow him into his hearse. I hesitated but he just nudged me into the passenger side. The hearse smelled like that new smell of death. Flowers. Satin. Wood. Powder. Not the rotting smell of death that's been around for some time. We drove to a D.D. meeting where I saw many people with their drinking under control. People approached me, reached out, welcomed me and shook my hand. Then I thought, oh no, a cult! But it wasn't. In fact it was better than the Catholic stuff that was rammed down my throat and had left me numb, like a two-by-four to the head from a God I thought was punishing. Holy smoke. Holy clutter. Smoke and clang clanging. I don't blame God though. No way.

Later, the undertaker drove me and the dead body home. We stopped in front of my house. The undertaker leaned back and half-opened the coffin lid. And he told me that the guy in the back could be me. I turned and looked at the corpse's rubbery, white-washed face and the stale flower smell wasn't so bad after all.

Outside, a dog barked its life at the sky."

Sofa Song

"I fix sofas and chairs for a living and I can build an easy chair from scratch. All I need are wood and material, a few nails, lots of staples, a couple of tools and I can shape something that will make your back feel like it's being held in the arms of your lover.

Anyway, last week I was so drunk and in the middle of a job. I sat my baby son inside the frame of the chair figuring he'd think he was in a playpen or something. Gave him his bottle and teddy bear for company. Then I had another drink and completely forgot about my little guy. Before I knew it I was done. Something wasn't right. I upholstered my son inside. Stapled everything shut and then his cry came from behind the fabric. I panicked. Thought I was hearing voices. Thought it was the child I had aborted four years ago, the voice that won't let go of me. Soon, I noticed my son was missing. I looked everywhere but couldn't find him. Took another shot of rum to help make the voice clearer. Then it suddenly hit me! Boy, you've never seen upholstery being ripped off a sofa chair so fast. I scooped out my son. Held him in my arms like a lost heart. Then I had another couple of stiff shots. When my boy stopped crying, he smiled in my arms and then tapped on my rum bottle, as if this were all a song to him."

Rum And Clothes

"Haven't changed clothes in a week. I'm starting to stink, like some of the men I've had. Must be growing a new skin too.

I fill my bathtub with warm water. No soap. Climb in with all my clothes still on. The phone rings. Jump out of the tub. Slosh to the phone. It's Room Service. Yes, I still want that bottle of white rum. Now. Thank you.

A knock at the door. I'm soaked. I wrap a blanket around me. Go to the door. Pay for the white rum. Head back to the bathtub. Open a window. Open the bottle. Take a swig. Gently place it on the floor beside the tub. Stand up. Climb out of the tub. Fling the blanket out the window, as if it were the most nauseous of all my skins. Climb back into the tub. Remove my blouse. My skirt. My slip. Fling each out the window. Do the same with my panty hose. My bra. My panties. I imagine birds swaying and the pigeons turning white again. I see a traffic cop down below nearly choking on his whistle. My skirt draped over his head, like a crumpled hat. My bra hanging from one of his ears to remind him that my breasts are so big that he could put one in his ear and one in his mouth and phone home. Blouse on his shoulders. Blanket over one arm. Panty hose over the other. His whistle wrapped in my panties. My slip covering his shoes, like a tiny satin cloud. A noonday store mannequin. Traffic gone mad.

I empty the bathtub. Order two more bottles. Splash rum all over myself. Take another belt. Light a match. Light another match. Light a third."

Sparrow

"I once saw a sparrow in my backyard feasting on old berries. After three or four pecks and swallows, the bird became more and more unsure of its spider walk. Soon, I saw the sparrow staggering across the grass, as if it were in a cartoon animal which had just been shot. First time I ever saw a sparrow stagger. Its song was broken and it stumbled into the fence and bushes. Then, it somehow moved out to the center of the lawn and fell to its knees in the wet, wet grass. Half-digested berries spurted up from the sparrow's throat, like a miniature volcano. I swear I heard the bird sing that it wanted to die right there. And the bird's name became caked on the grass, like a designer headstone. Finally, the sparrow keeled over and died on its own name. Imagine dying on the letters of your name. I'd better wait an extra couple of days to mow my backyard, out of respect for another dead drunk who could be me or you."

Faces and Choices

"I had no choice. Either get treatment via The Employee Assistance Program or get a pink slip and hit the bricks. So here I was this brilliant, hard-nosed researcher heading off to a treatment center. Everyone at work was so relieved that I heard they all undid the top two buttons of their shirts, dresses or blouses to celebrate my decision. They even had a face-loosening contest and the office became one huge lung when I left. My boss later told me he tried everything to win the contest but couldn't because I had caused him to have an office face that was tighter than a bull's ass at branding time, a face that hurt for days when it discovered it could relax.

I may be a drunk but I'm certainly no fool. Stupidity was a way of life for me but I wanted my job back afterwards. Even if it meant being locked up for thirty days. I left behind the pictures of all the expensive cars I dreamed of owning because my dreams didn't work anymore. Best to leave them hanging on my office walls where they could never come true. In the treatment center, I was told that, in a few tomorrow's, I'd be able to make choices again. And my first visitor was my boss. Should have seen his face when he saw me looking him straight in the eye."

Cough Syrup And Rye

"Ran out of places to hide my booze. I tried the closet. My dresser drawers. In the bottom of the dirty laundry. Under a ceiling tile in the basement. Behind a stereo speaker. In cupboards. In my winter boots. In the inside pocket of my ski jacket. In the fireplace. Under my old fur hat. You name it and I've used it.

The very best place was inside my cough syrup bottle and I left the bottle right there, in plain view of everyone, on the kitchen counter. Everyone in the house thought I had to take the cough syrup because of my chronic cough. Nobody questioned or touched my cough syrup. No one. And no one asked why I went back for seconds so often.

For some reason or other, one day my cough went away, and it certainly wasn't because of my health. My husband removed the bottle from the kitchen table and placed it in the medicine cabinet where all the other leftover bottles of cough medicine sat, like half-dressed people. Like me. But not for long. To bring back the cough, I started smoking again. Then, I made a fake call to the drugstore to have my prescription renewed.

ONE, TWO, THREE ON ME!"

The Man Who Lost His Teeth

"There I was in the bathroom after too many drinks, and my head kept spinning in and out of the mirror, like one of those tops. I nearly fell into the bathtub but my fall was broken by my grabbing onto the toilet bowl. Then, I threw up into the toilet. At least my aim was good. Couldn't stop. Soon, my dentures pushed their way out of my mouth and plopped into the toilet bowl. Too late. I flushed. Gone. Vomit and teeth. Blood.

A few people at the party tried to help me retrieve my dentures but…

A brush was stuffed into the hole but it couldn't do the job. So many drunken fingers and hands were poking into the hole at the same time. Drunk heroes. Never did get my teeth back. Nobody went to the toilet after that. Everyone left early. The host and hostess even let me sleep there overnight. There was still a lot of booze left but I didn't want to look greedy or maybe lose my tongue down the toilet too.

Next day, they called a plumber. After he had unscrewed the bowl from the floor, the plumber found the dentures lodged somewhere. No matter how many times they were washed and dried, I simply couldn't get those teeth back into my face. And my mouth just hung open in the morning sunlight, like a paper cup filled with cotton and air."

On The Rectory Roof

"We bring case after case after case of Molson's Export Ale up onto the roof of the rectory. A priest is giving a couple of us a going-away party but he warns us to not stand too close to the edge in case. Especially after a few beer. We drink and drink until about ten o'clock, the priest somehow gets his Harley Davidson up onto the roof. Everyone takes a little turn around the roof.

A man and woman each leave their spouses and climb down the attic opening to the bathroom. They meet face to face just outside the priest's bathroom and the man pulls her inside with him. They are all over each other, as if they'd never had sex in their lives. Furiously, they make love in the dark on the cold, hard bathroom floor. A goodbye present. The man flushes the toilet to make noise and hopes nobody is outside waiting. Unlocking the door, he looks out to see if anyone is there. Safe for now. He leaves first. She leaves two minutes later, making sure to count to one hundred and twenty before flushing the toilet a second time.

Later, back on the roof, the couple lets their sexy sweat blow off into the nighttime air, listen to the St Jean Baptist Day fireworks and watch the Harley drive circles around their passion. I knew though. I knew. I could smell the sex on them. In the distance, a cry is heard, as if the husband just found out and drove the Harley through a cloud.

Who does't believe my Harley story."

The Nowhere Ditch

"Yesterday, I woke up in my car in a nowhere ditch. Blackout. Where did I come from? Who was I? My wallet was empty. My credit cards were gone. I had peed my pants. My face felt like a muddy sidewalk and my eyes belonged to a dead man.

All started two days ago when my friend asked me to go for a few beer. He was getting married in a few days and wanted me to be his best man. I couldn't believe it. He had been sober for nearly three years and figured a beer or two wouldn't hurt. So I had a few and a few more with him. Two days forgotten in broken glass talk.

Now we're both at this Don't Drink meeting. People tell us that the door swings both ways. Some of us need to go out drinking again. Get it out of our systems. Practice some more. Be brought to our knees. The sleeve on my friend's black sweater is soaked with tears and looks like a swollen hour hand on a clock. His wedding is tomorrow.

After the D.D. meeting, I'm going straight home. See if I can locate those two days on my calendar. Those lost ditch days. Maybe my car remembers something."

Seven Eggs

"I am invited to my friend's house to help clean his backyard. My friend's father is downstairs checking the homemade wine in his barrels. I didn't have any breakfast before coming and the warning sounds in my stomach get louder.

We work hard and an hour later, all the leaves are raked into piles of sun. My friend's father has a little wine left in an old barrel and he gives it to us in tumbler glasses. Down the hatch it goes, the thirst that strong for anything wet. Then, we go inside for some breakfast.

At the kitchen table is a plate filled with seven yellow-eyed eggs staring back at me and moving in circles, together and then alone. Wine eyes. Everyone around the table watches and listens to me count each of the seven eggs on my plate, but there are only two eggs there, my friend's mother keeps telling me. Yolks float across each other like blurred movie characters. I stab and stab with my fork but cannot find the real eggs. Laughter. Laughter. I better lie down for a while. Right now. More laughter. Two egg yolks shaking on my plate, like the eyes of a clown. I hear my friend's mother say that if I think I have too much on my plate right now, I probably do."

Take Me Back To Life

"I disappeared for three years. Lived on the river bank. Everyone thought I was dead, except for one sister. She kept looking for me until finally, she got a lead from a halfway house. Someone told her to look for me under the Langevin Bridge. And she actually came down to the bridge and found me. All of my under the bridge friends thought she was from another planet because of her neat, clean clothes, her perfect hair and her business-like voice. My sister always spoke with no feeling in her voice so why should she be different today. Dressed in every cliché of poverty, I also had long, matted, filthy black hair, no teeth and sores on my neck and face. Yet, my sister didn't care the least. She scooped me up in her arms, like she did when I was her little brother. Amazing. I cried. And cried. I remember her calm voice asking me why the reds on the whites of my eyes were deepening in color. She said she was taking me back to life and I had no idea where that was. Maybe, I should just die here. If I stay, insanity. Better leave. No, I'm not worried about going crazy now that my big sister is here. When we got to her car, she very cooley opened the door for me, walked around to the driver's side, unlocked her door and then climbed into the driver's seat. Finally, she turned on the ignition and I watched her body tremble in so many tears, I thought she'd melt. So, I reached over and held her in my arms, like I wanted to do all my life. I could taste the salt on her face. Feel its sting. The crazy salt.

Last week, I think it was, a friend told me that crazy was a place to go."

Whiskey Pain

"After a while ya gotta let go of it all. My husband died six months ago. Killed himself with a shotgun. Took one right in the mouth. The shape on the other side of his head looked like a big 'M'. His note said I never gave him a chance to talk and this was his revenge. The big 'M' was for my mouth because he said that I'd never give my mouth a rest, even when his head was turned. Of course, this was all bullshit! If anything, he talked way too much himself, especially when he was drinking. But I have to let his lie go. All of it. Let my Greater Spirit take over from me. Otherwise, my husband will be living rent-free inside me. Everyone says that I have to leave the pain in its place. I'd love to hear my husband's advice right now. He often thought he was God when he was drinking. One minute he thought he was at the top of the heap and the next he'd disappear into the bottom of the pile. I'd like to hear his final words. Listen to the times his pain was so bad that he threatened to cut his ears off. Covered his eyes. Bent over, head on his knees. Cried whiskey tears down to his ankles. Even his shoes were filled with his whiskey me, me, me's.

They say he wished upon a glass star."

Lawn Mower Night

"It was seven o'clock on a September, Friday night. Between sips of rye, my mother tells me I should be out having fun. Yet, she just told me a few minutes ago to mow the lawn. Then she tells me to stop the lawn mower and go out for some Friday night good times. She gives me ten bucks. Says I should be with my friends. So, being a good son, I stop mowing, pocket the ten bucks and park the lawn mower against the house in the back, promising to finish the job tomorrow. Then, I go inside to wash up and change.

Soon, I leave and go out with some friends. Go shoot pool. Hang out. Spend the ten bucks.

At eleven-thirty, I'm back home and hear the lawn mower in the backyard. I walk around to the back. See the back porch light on. See my mother gripping a bottle of rye in one hand and pushing the lawn mower with the other. I ask her what's she's doing, mowing the lawn at eleven-thirty at night. She scowls at me muttering that she had asked me earlier to cut the grass and I just took off like that with my friends and she can't count on me for anything."

Famous Player

"Played bass in an all-girl band. That's how it all began. Wasn't long before I got real good at it. Soon after, I was asked to join a better band with me as the only female.

At the time, my mother ran a boarding-house in Saskatoon and her dream was to see me become rich and famous so she could dump the boarding-house. Well, she let me hit the road and our band headed to Le Pas, Manitoba. What a dump of a hotel! Then other small towns. Then cities. Played all the bars. Lots of booze. Lots of messing around with other men, even though I had recently married the keyboard player in our band. My husband thought we had a marriage made in heaven. Somehow, I always found a way to slip away with another man for a couple of hours every few days. Our drummer felt really good. Strong arms. Great wrists. Guess I really needed to have another man in my arms. A man who fit differently. Know what I mean? Of course you do.

One night my mother showed up for our big gig when we were playing back home in Saskatoon. Imagine, she left all her boarders alone to check up on me. And she would never leave her boarding-house when it was loaded with roomers. By this time I was working in my fifth band, one of the top groups in Western Canada. I was so drunk that I sang backup harmony off-key and people noticed. Even played my bass off-key. The band stopped playing. I kept going, as if my life depended on it. Our manager shut off my amp and fired me on the spot. Right away, my mother climbed on-stage, asked the manager to look up and then rammed a microphone between his legs. Should have heard his voice! Worse than mine. Then my mom ever so gently, lifted my guitar from my arms, as if it were a dangerous toy I might fall asleep on, and took me home to her boarding-house where she said I could learn how to be famous all over again."

My Hair Is Older Than Me

"Why is my hair so neat but fake? What do you mean it looks like a shrinking bird's nest? Because it's old, that's why, and I'm saving to buy a new hairpiece. So lay off. Leave my head alone! Okay? And when you go home tonight to say your prayers, ask for brains. Got it? Now, let me get on with my story.

I used to be brakeman for the C.P.R.. I'd drink rye from my thermos while on the job until one night I made a mistake and a boxcar filled with empty cans was derailed. The doors flew open and there were bright, new cans everywhere. Looked like someone planted tin stars in the ground. I stopped drinking right then and there. White-knuckled it for five weeks until I couldn't stand it anymore and got my hands on a couple of mickeys of rye. And that night I nearly wrecked an entire freight train as it left Calgary on its way to Thunder Bay. My boss ordered me to get some help or get fired. He could have fired me right on the spot but he didn't. Told me I was making everyone nervous. So I went into a treatment program and then started attending D.D. meetings. Even met a woman in D.D. and fell in love. You know how alcoholics are always falling in love. We soon got married and there we were — two recovering drunks under the same roof. What a house. Today, I only imagine a boxcar being derailed. The worst train wreck is now caused, I think, when I dream I am cheating, that I never stopped drinking, that I'm still at it. When I wake up the next morning, it takes my head so long to dry from all the sweating. That's why my piece looks older than me. Takes awhile before I can put on my hair for the day. And when I finally slip it on, I pray like a fool that what I'll see today is true."

Steel And Education

"Drank nearly all of a forty-ouncer of rye when the pain was too much. Placed the barrel of a thirty-eight into my mouth to kill the too-much-pain. Loneliness. Fear. Resentment. Depression. Had to separate this aching from me. Didn't matter if I died. The pain had to go first I figured. Wish I could have it pulled, like a bad tooth. With the gun in my mouth, I hesitated and thought what if I didn't do the job right and the pain afterwards was worse than it is now? What if I hit the kitchen floor and was only nearly dead? What's the purpose of being nearly dead? What about that new pain? Twice I withdrew the gun from my mouth and then slid it back in immediately afterwards. Good thing I didn't pull the trigger. Good thing. Still, after fourteen years of not drinking I can still taste the cold, bitter taste of steel in my mouth and my tongue curling around the hardness. It's a good reference point for me whenever pain tries to take over. Last night my sponsor said, that besides being an alcoholic, I had too much education and I think too much. Then I asked him why was it always the guys with little education who said that."

Doing The Warming

"At the funeral parlor, I wanted to see my dead mother right away and try really hard to feel something for her but the funeral director told me she wasn't ready yet. They still had to make up her face. Put in her teeth. Fix her hair. Clothes. Everything. But I insisted on seeing her right away. Forget the makeup, the coffin look. I pushed my way into a back room where they worked on the dead bodies to make them look good. Saw my mother. Ran to hold her cold, cold hand. Forced myself to feel something for her by pretending that I was watching one of those TV shows where the mother was a special person dying from Cancer. Forced myself hard. Posed as her son. Played possum with my love for her. And her hand became warmer and warmer. I stroked the mothering in her pores. Smelled her blood. Heard a slight exhaling. Felt more warming. When I pointed this out to the funeral director, he reminded me that I was probably breathing for two and it was my hand doing all the warming.

I was ready."

Tools

"Whenever I get drunk, I imitate tools. My friends especially love when I become an electric drill or screwdriver. They laugh and laugh and tell me I sound exactly like the tool. The sounds work better the more I drink. When I do a table-saw cutting through a two-by-four, my friends make faces like they are in pain. I can cut up anyone, anytime.

Last week at a party, I was an electric screwdriver and I twisted my head into a sofa chair that was occupied by an incredibly beautiful, blue-eyed woman. Well, my friends nearly fell out of their chairs and choked on their beer and booze. The woman just slid over to one side in the sofa chair and ignored me while sipping her drink. Then, she told me I must enjoy my insanity and that she's working hard at imitating a human being. Imagine, she would not laugh no matter how hard I tried to sound like an electric screwdriver. Maybe it was her looks that did it. Maybe, it was me.

Whenever I get drunk, I imitate tools."

Cancel The Morphine

"I've been hooked on one thing or another all my life. It all started with green lollipops when I was five. Next, it was chocolate and Pepsi. After, it was caffeine. Then, booze and marijuana. I'm addicted to addiction. Now, the day before I die, I am swallowing with the look of a woman who has just gulped an umbrella. But I am sober. Alive. Almost clean. Almost. Except for morphine which I need to kill the last hours of my pain. The doctors say I have about forty-eight hours to live. How can those people tell? Aw, let my boobs sag, will ya. Let my ass head south. Who cares anymore? Let me go! Cancel the morphine. I want to die completely clean and sober. Do you hear me? Cancel the morphine. Now!"

Not Much More To Say

"I take my son out to buy the week's groceries because he insists that he come along in case. We stop at the liquor store anyway and I buy just a six-pack of beer. Of course, I promise my son that was all I plan to drink this weekend.

When we get home, my boy goes out to play. As soon as I hear the front door slam shut, I call Dial-A-Bottle and order two bottles of vodka and another six-pack of beer. The booze comes while my son is playing in a neighbor's backyard. I hide the vodka behind the couch and the second six-pack in the vegetable tray because I know how much my kid hates vegetables and he'd never look there for snacks or anything.

When my son comes home about an hour later, I'm already into the vodka and have had two beer. One beer is missing from the vegetable tray and one from the six-pack on the coffee table that I bought with my son. All my boy sees is the one empty beer can. I'm starting to feel no pain and my son is wondering why I got so drunk so fast on so little. He comes close. Smells my breath. Moves away. Picks up the empty beer can. Flings it against a window because I'm a drunk of a mother and I can con anyone.

The doorbell rings."

Baby Brush

"I'm at the airport just being a good young mother going on a trip when I feel I have to brush my baby's hair. Even though she has barely any hair. I brush and part. Brush and part. After I hand the baby and brush to my eight-year-old son and ask him to continue. I dip into my purse and pull out a perfume bottle. I look over one shoulder. Then the other. I look to the left, the right. I unscrew the bottle cap and take a good swig. I screw the cap back on and slip the little bottle back into my purse, exhaling with a smile as wide as the bench we're on. We're about to board our flight. Someone calls us first. We get in line. I take my infant back and ask for the baby brush. I part the angel hair on my baby's head. Part. Brush. Part. Brush. Our line gets shorter. The parting nears. My son's eyes move up and down, across and back, like some kind of video game. Eyes looking at everyone but us, as if my boy were measuring the seconds until I ask him to hold the baby again. Behind us I hear only other mothers."

Just Gimme My Rye

"You think that because I'm his mother, he'd understand. I only want him to stop at a liquor store and pick up a bottle of rye for me.That's not too much to ask from a son, is it? It's the dead of winter. Nearly thirty below but feels colder. Yea, yea, I know. He tells me he has to get back home soon for an important phone call. And he needs to get some groceries first. Food. Food. What's more important anyway? Now he says he'll just drop me off at the liquor store and I can buy my own bottle. Because he stopped drinking and joined that outfit called Don't Drink, he won't go into any liquor stores. I don't want to stop drinking. I don't have a problem with booze. Imagine him just dropping me off in this ice cold weather. The nerve of that guy and he's supposed to be my son!

Later, I'm still waiting in line to get my rye when my son honks his horn and motions me to get into the car. I won't leave this line until I've got that twenty-sixer in my hands. He'll have to wait. More honking. More gesturing. I can almost hear him yelling behind the windshield. Then he gets out of the car and slams the door. His face is a red boxing glove. He's coming this way, exhaling, exhaling, stomping through the crusty snow."

Skipping

"At the Don't Drink meeting, someone says I look exactly like Santa Claus without the red suit. I squeeze myself into a chair and feel like I'm ready to doze off. Patches of sweat spread under my blue T-shirt look, like warm lakes. My brow shrinks under more beads of sweat when I tell everyone how tired I am from working on my back deck. My head droops just as I grab my styrofoam cup of coffee and spill some on my lap. I don't feel a thing. Asleep. Dead asleep. Even with hot coffee on my crotch. Feels like pee. Warm pee. I am in a room filled with two-by-four's, nails, hammers, and saws.

Paramedics arrive. They inject me with glucose. I awake. Say this has never happened to me at a D.D. meeting. Diabetes. Good thing I haven't had a drink in over twenty years. Must of skipped supper tonight. Must have skipped something. Can't remember. God, I don't feel like Santa Claus and I need a shower."

Go To Sleep

"Every night that husband of mine keeps telling me to get to bed but I want to stay up, have a few drinks and read my Agatha Christie book. And each night I tell him to go to sleep, to leave me alone with Agatha Christie. Rye and water. Just a couple of rye and water's. You know. Helps me sleep better. Helps me sleep in too. Let him get up and make porridge for the kids in the morning. Let him do it. I gotta do the laundry, the cleaning, the cooking and all kinds of other things. Go to bed? No I won't. Agatha Christie's not done with me yet. Time for another rye and water. Why won't he let up? I'm not going to bed for awhile yet. Bet he's just horny. My thirst is more important. Go to sleep. Go to sleep. Go hushaby your hard-on."

Bar Scam

"Cheapest way in the world to get drunk in a busy bar. My buddy and I do it all the time. We watch for a couple to go to the dance floor which means they are leaving their drinks unattended. One of us acts as a wall and the other gulps down the couple's drinks. We take turns. One is the shielder. One is the gulper. Works best in crowded bars. But tonight while my buddy is the shielder and me the gulper, I come across a drink that has dentures floating in it. Smart ass. He or she must have known. So to thank him or her, I drop my half-smoked cigarette into the glass and watch the ashes swirl around the teeth like tiny, black claws. I also let a burnt match float above it all. Finally, I write a thank-you note on the inside of a matchbook and leave it hanging from the glass. Then, we move to another table and wait for the couple to return. Wait for the glass to reach those toothless lips in the disco dark."

The First

"My home is now a park bench here in Honolulu. I used to own a huge advertising business in Boston. Paid myself a quarter million dollars a year. Became a big shot. A high roller. Got so busy that I stopped going to D.D. meetings after nine years of sobriety. One day I was invited to lunch and had a rye and ginger before lunch, just like that. I had another and another and another and no lunch. Didn't leave that restaurant–bar until closing time. Then, I went on a two week drinking spree and wound up in jail. Wasn't long before I lost my business, my wife, my children, the house, the two cars in the garage, everything. Ended up on this park bench between two other drunks. Don't even ask how I got to Hawaii because I haven't a clue. Now I pay myself nothing. Absolutely nothing. And for what? For what? Because that first drink killed me. Not the third. Not the sixth. Not the twentieth. The first. And now, each morning I get on my knees and pray to the surf rolling in off Waikiki. At first, all I heard were Beach Boy, Dan Ho or Jan and Dean songs. But always, I keep praying, praying until I hear no music at all."

Noisy Sun

"I live in my van and take showers at the beach nearly every morning. I used to think I was Richie Valens performing in a rock band on stage in front of fifteen thousand fans. Listen. Listen. They are here for me. Me. I sing better than Richie. See that guy over there? Well, he used to play bass in my band. Ask him when he wakes up. He'll tell you how good I was. La Bamba. La Bamba. Listen to me sing. Listen. La La Bamba. La La Bamba. You like? You like? And look at that Waikiki sun coming up! Yea, even the morning sun is brought to life by my voice. The sun yells. Yesterday, another homeless guy told me that when the sun yells, it's really God shouting back my pain at me. Listen to that crowd! They love me! They love me! Yea! Yea! Watch me bow to the sun. Man, I've worked up a sweat. It's time. Time for a morning shower and then back to my dressing-room van for a nap. Not easy living on the road. But I do what I gotta do. I owe it to my fans. And it is only when I nap that the noise goes away.

I live in my van and I used to think myself crazy."

Oregon Waitress

"Once I used to be a blonde waitress in a small Oregon town. Men would always just squeeze by me so they could brush by my ass on their way to the washroom. Sometimes, I gave them a slap. Other times, I ignored them by accidentally spilling hot coffee on their crotches. I was that sexy, that beautiful. I guess. I used to steal money from the till. Just a little at a time. And booze too. But then I got pregnant and was in a marriage with a man I hated because he only used that little head between his legs to think. One day I left him and his little head and started going to Don't Drink meetings.

I still feel very blonde, very sexy, very beautiful even though my hair is back to its sandy brown color. And my daughter is now nine. She is more gorgeous than I ever was. I'm not waiting for the day when she feels as sexy as I do though. One day I'll tell her exactly what booze did to me and what my hair used to look like. All I can do is share. I can't control how she thinks, how she feels. So what she thinks or feels about me is really none of my business. Feelings have no brains anyway."

Scooter Man

"They call me Scooter Man here in Waikiki.

To celebrate your two years of sobriety, I brought you a couple of gifts. Two hula girls. Wind-up toys really. Just for a joke. Any feminists here object? No? Good. What's that? You've got wind-up boys of your own? I bet you do. Ha! Let me get the gifts from my scooter.

Oops! Sorry. Looks like they fell off my scooter on the way here, so they'll be arriving late to celebrate your second birthday. Both girls are here right now, in spirit. Listen to their grass skirts. Listen to the surf. Now, I'll play my ukulele. Hey, look! The hula girls have arrived, limping a little but here anyhow. Watch them wave with armfuls of sun. Look at those palm trees twisting, turning, toasting you. But, stay humble. Know why those coconut trees have tin wrapped around them half-way up? To keep rats from nesting at the top. Happy Birthday to you. Happy Birthday to you. Happy Birthday. Happy Birthday. Happy Birthday to you – from The Scooter Man, who wishes you well in keeping the rats out of your hair."

Harley Davidson Woman

"What do you mean by asking if I have a licence to drive this wheelchair? You trying to be funny? Watch it! Next time I'll run you over! Any more smartass comments like that and I'll take your kneecaps off with one push of a button!

I like being dressed from head-to-toe in black leather. They say my hair is as grey as cigarette ashes. See these wrinkles – think of them as highways running beside one another. Don't mess with me or my leather cap! I was riding Harley's before your father and mother rode each other to make you. Do you like the way my leather shines in the sun? When I was drinking, I couldn't afford a fancy wheelchair like this, never mind the Harley duds. Used to wear jeans, a jean jacket, a T-shirt from Wal-Mart and black leather boots. Had to turn four tricks as a wheelchair hooker just to buy the boots. Thought all I needed was one or two tricks but those john's were tighter than an administrator's ass at the end of a day. Now sobriety has given me my dream back and I have the money for not only the fancy wheelchair but also all this real leather. So, you want to apologize to me? Sure. Sure. Do you drive a bike? You do? Tell me... tell me how it feels?"

Punch Out

"Used to punch out everyone when I drank. For every punch I got back, the person got two more from me. Didn't matter if it was a man or another woman, or if the person was six foot six and weighed two fifty. Once I hit a guy in a bar so hard with an empty beer glass that I thought his nose would spring out from the back of his head and then look like one of those Christmas tree decorations. Another time, I smacked a woman so hard in the belly that I thought she'd have to wear her belly button as a nose-ring.

Haven't stopped rubbing the knuckles on my right hand for years. Helps when I curl and uncurl the fingers, one at a time. Smiling helps too. Now, I only swing my fist at the sky. Don't have to smack anyone anymore. Ever since I stopped drinking and started coming to these Don't Drink meetings, I only punch out the sky – a cloud, the sun, the moon. Helps me to remember where I came from and who I was. Slowly, my three ex-husbands are feeling safer when any of them comes within striking distance.

Yesterday, I saw my five sons all together for the first time in years. Each one of them stayed at least an arm's length away but the loving will happen when it's supposed to. At least they all say I look saner and my hands stay longer in my pockets the more I hear that. Not a bad start, isn't it? Isn't it? What do you mean you have nothing to say about all this?"

Bikini Colors

"Look at me.

I'll be sixty-years old in three days and I still enjoy wearing a bikini. Do you like these frills around my waist? Sure you do. My ex-husband once said I looked like a shrivelled-up department store mannequin dressed to go nowhere. I guess that's why he's my ex. But I love all these colors. Maybe this sounds corny but the colors make me feel grateful for being alive because I don't drink anymore. Like signs or signals. Know what I mean? And I want you all to notice that my bikini has ten colors. This morning I decided that each color represents the ten people I've known who died from booze because they just couldn't stop drinking. Each of these people thought he or she was cured or were too busy to learn how to live with some kind of emotional sobriety. Now, I'm not taking their inventories or anything. We know what happens when we think we are cured. Puppies. We're all like puppies making messes around the house and somebody up there just smiles warmly at us, as if each pile of poop was a just a forgivable shortcoming.We go out there and think we can drink like anyone else. How many here want to either die or end up in a loony bin? Those are the choices. Please don't choose. Don't choose anything. I'm running out of colors. What's that you say? There are only two colors? Black and white. Well...yes and no.

Look at me."

Letters On The Windshield

"I was driving up a steep hill in the middle of a snowstorm, hungover like crazy from the night before. Didn't think I'd make it to the top. Too slippery. I almost didn't. Stopped just about at the top and slid back half-way down. Good thing it was five in the morning. I was heading to work on a Sunday. Something I rarely do. Special overtime job. Hardly no one on the road. No parked vehicles. Lucky for me. I stepped on the gas again and nudged my way to the top. Made it. Barely. And I was sweating twice as hard because of the hangover. My head throbbed so bad I thought my brain would burst out of my head, like a rocket going nowhere, and smack against the windshield. Instead, I threw up against my closed window, thinking it was open. You can just imagine what I looked like. That was it! I'd had it with booze. Looked up on my windshield and a message was written in snowflakes: D.D. There it was as plain as day. Two letters. D.D. I know. I know. This all sounds like a TV show called Touched By Something or a movie but what can I say. I know what I saw. That was the day I stopped drinking. And that night I went to my very first Don't Drink meeting. It saved my ass and I don't care how I got the message. The point is, I couldn't handle the hills anymore. Even in good weather."

Moving Furniture

"Both my husband and I were heavy drinkers. He'd go out to bars and I'd do it alone at home. I was at the point where going anywhere just terrified me. My hubby hadn't arrived there yet in his drinking. And when I drank, I moved everything. Often. I'd change the living room furniture. Shuffle everything into different rooms. The more I drank, the more I shuffled. Then I'd do our bedroom. Sometimes I'd stumble into the kitchen and move all the plates, glasses, knives and forks. No matter where I put things, I had to be satisfied, it had to feel right. There were times when I'd move all the bedroom furniture into the living room and vice-versa. Once, I slid our bed into the kitchen and when my husband came home he turned on the kitchen light and found me dead asleep with a food processor cradled in one of my arms and a stainless steel salad bowl in the other.

Sometimes he came home drunk and banged into the fridge thinking our bed was there. Don't ask me where I got the strength to move those heavy things because I haven't a clue. Or he'd stumble into the living room hoping to crash on the couch but end up falling on the kitchen table. Occasionally, he'd be in the kitchen opening and slamming doors and drawers looking for a glass or a knife to spread his crunchy peanut butter on Ritz Crackers. You know what those munchies are like. Anyhow, last night he wrapped his finger in a paper towel so he could scoop peanut butter out of the jar. He knows how I feel when he uses a dirty, bare finger."

With My Stepdaughter

"She was seventeen and I took her to the bar one night. Afterwards we got a little too friendly and my stepdaughter got pregnant by me. I knew it was going to happen right then and there for some reason. Well, she had the baby and my new wife never found out that I was the father until one night I was working my shift as a bus driver. I was so drunk I didn't remember going to or from work. I remember my new wife yelling at me that not only was I a no-good drunk but also a sick man who screws his stepdaughter and gets her pregnant. And I thought she never knew. Me and that woman lasted exactly twenty months together. Then she kicked me out and I got an apartment of my own. Great! Now I could drink all I wanted and no one would bother me. But it got worse and worse. I pulled my phone out of the wall. Stopped answering the door. Mail piled up. I wrote the word DECEASED on each of my unpaid bills and sent them back. I drank and drank until the day I saw babies pouring out of the walls. My babies. Each of them pad-padding towards me and holding a lit wooden match in each hand."

And Stuff Like That

"Once at a party, we all had to guess which food each of us looked like and someone said I looked like a huge dill pickle with bleach blonde hair. But, I'm still sane and sober. For today anyhow. I have to get on my knees every morning. I have to surrender my day because that's how I win and stuff like that. I'll be okay if I ask my Greater Spirit for help and stuff like that. If during the day I run into trouble, I can go into a private place, like a bathroom or closet, get on my knees and start the day all over again, even if I really am a giant dill pickle with blonde hair. At least, I'm a lucky dill pickle. And at the end of the day, I just have to show my gratitude by giving thanks on my knees. God knows we need help and stuff like that.

There is no stuff like that in that so-called normal world. Normies. Ha! I know of so many people who could use D.D. so they can learn how to live with themselves and others and stuff like that. Saw a cartoon in the paper the other day that showed a huge convention hall with a banner stuck to the wall saying: CONVENTION OF NORMAL ANONYMOUS and you know what — there were only three people in the audience.

I know a short woman at work who has long, stringy black hair and who walks down the hallway every morning making sure her footsteps are heard by everyone. Her father died last year at the age of forty-nine and he spoke a lot about breaking up with his wife, even on his deathbed and stuff like that. Seems he loved the Rolling Stones. The woman at work needs to be right and has two or three other women who she controls like toys and stuff like that. They follow her around like she's the smartest and toughest woman they ever met. Bet she's never been a kid in her life and if she ever laughed… well… I wouldn't want to be in her underwear and stuff like that."

Training

"I had to replace my seeing eye dog after I sobered up. The dog only knew how to get me to three places: the liquor store, the bar and home. They say it would take too long to break the dog of his old habits and teach him how to get me to a Don't Drink meeting. The agency that provided these dogs reminded me that I'd better stay sober, at least for the new dog's sake because it takes about two to three years to train these animals. In the meantime, I had Don't Drink members drive me to meetings while I waited. Believe it or not, that first dog tried to teach me how to feel when it brought me to the liquor store, the bar and home. He never gave up on me. Makes me wonder if the dog had a heart in each paw. Four hearts. Yea, that's it! But at the time of my drinking, my own heart couldn't feel for anyone or anything outside of me. Almost seems like I had to use the Sears Catalogue or something and phone in to order for a new heart. To start feeling again, I have to stay sober. One day at a time. Not that I want to bleed all over everyone. Imagine what my new dog will teach me. Think of me on all fours."

One Morning I Awoke

"One morning I woke up in a place called Flagship, Montana I think it was. Only problem was that Flagship didn't have an airport or a train station or a bus depot and I didn't remember how I got there. I felt inside my pockets for some kind of a ticket stub. Maybe, I had taken a bus there. Nothing. I searched for car keys to see if I had driven there somehow. Nothing. No wallet. I had no suitcase with me. Nobody in town knew how I got there. So I sat under a statue for hours until my head cleared and it was then I remembered the gorgeous redhead I met in the bar who took me for a drive. I remember the strong flavor of cigarettes in her mouth and her tongue moving like a nicotine snake. Then there was the smell of smoke on her skin and in her hair. We stopped on the road so I could have a pee. I heard the striking, then the whoosh of a match for another cigarette. I remember the sound of her laughter bouncing off the sky when I told her I was writing a novel with my pee in the dust. After that, I don't remember a thing."

Spiderman

"Some people call me Spiderman because of my Spiderman tattoo. But I don't think the real Spiderman had a red beard, wore dark sunglasses, shaved his head, weighed two-fifty and had a tattoo completely covering his head and face. Nor did Spiderman dress totally in denim, like I do. Some people say I look like a giant comic book character and belong in Hollywood where I could save lives in biker movies. Do you like my earrings? My black leather boots? Know why I want to save lives? My counsellor tells me I do it for one reason only: I want to bank what people owe me. The usual drunk reason.

Doesn't matter how I look. I will not take that first drink. For today anyhow. I'm just here to be of use to someone besides myself. Bet the real Spiderman wasn't a recovering drunk. Bet he was a Boy Scout who overdosed on milk and cookies and his entire life experience was playing in his backyard. The only backyard I had was the one I saw from a second floor apartment bedroom window, a backyard patched with yellow grass and rats searching for a sundown meal and there was no way I could change any of that. Yet, I have to remember that Spiderman has a right to run around all day in tights. By the way, are his comic books still available?"

Unlearning My Whole Life

"When I was a young boy, my parents said I had to have strong willpower. Always. So I did. If things didn't go my way, I'd let the world know. I remember when I wanted this red bicycle. I was desperate! Used to go visit that bike in the store, as if the bike were a new right or left arm I needed badly. I'd stare at it. Talk to it. Walk by it maybe fifty times. Run my hand across the chrome handlebars and feel the cool metal. Smell the newness of the leather seat, the rubber tires. Even the fenders had the smell of new tin. Dream of riding it right out of the store. I pushed and pushed my parents until finally they gave in and bought the bike for me. They said it counted as both a birthday and Christmas present. Ha!

Same thing happened with everything else. Fighting. Always fighting. On my first day at school I got into trouble because I expected both the teacher and every other kid in my class to do things my way. Always trouble. And now I have to learn how to lose so I can win. Hope I don't sound like a shrink because we all know how useless they can be when it comes to sobering up but... it's like unlearning my whole life so I can get rid of those emotional handcuffs that chain me to me.

What's that you say? You rode the same bike too?"

In My Basement

"Used to be a mole in my basement and drink my brain cells dry.

After awhile, I unplugged the phone and pulled the curtains closed. I didn't want to see or talk to anyone. Just drink. Had me one of those Texas mickeys that was almost as tall as a floor lamp. Enough rye for an army of me's. Then, I would watch the silent, empty screen for awhile. See my face in the glass. Watch the red eyes looking back at me, like cracked traffic lights. See the glass become one eye. After, I turned on my TV and watched it for hours. Blur. Couldn't tell the comedies from the serious stuff after awhile. Next, I'd find everything funny. I'd laugh at innocent people being shot and killed during a bank robbery. One time I saw a man having his right hand chopped off at the wrist and I laughed that I wouldn't expect that guy to get a grip on himself for some time. Nothing made me cry on TV. Nothing made me angry. Yet, after turning off my TV, I'd start resenting everyone I knew and didn't know, including the me who laughed at the guy who had his hand chopped off. I'd even drink at each and every person I resented. I drank at myself. Do you think the people I resented cared? I doubt it. Had to tell them to go live inside someone else's head.

Used to be a mole in my basement and drink my brain cells dry."

Around The Jukebox

"There were eight soldiers standing around the jukebox, drinking beer and telling stories, laughing and planning the next song. Then all of a sudden, BOOM! The jukebox blew up in their faces. The sudden screams of death. Fingers, hands, arms, legs, eyes, noses, heads and other body parts were scattered all over the place. Same with steel and glass pieces. Black vinyl confetti and blood covered everything. Seems that an enemy soldier had snuck in the night before and planted a bomb in the jukebox. It was set to go off at eleven that night.The enemy knew. Two days later they even bragged about their 'Major Jukebox Victory' by dropping propaganda leaflets over our camp. Because I was the coroner but just another recovering drunk, I had to retrieve each body piece and match each with a body, a name, a soldier. I tried hard not to mix up parts in each of the body bags but... anything can happen. Anyhow, the parts were placed into their respective body bags and sent home. Never did hear from the families if they had received the wrong arm or leg or head. A colleague mentioned that maybe I had been a doctor long enough to imagine which part went with which. No way! It was like guessing the next song."

Blackout

"My patient begged me to operate on him but at the time, I needed a good drink first. I was already half in the bag but it wasn't enough for my doctoring confidence. I needed more booze. It was his intestines. There was something wrong. Pain. Fear. Something badly clogged. After telling my patient to hold on for a few seconds, I went back into my office and pulled out a vodka bottle, then poured myself a couple of stiff ones. After, I returned to the operating room with my hands as steady as the moon. The patient, who also happened to be a friend, forced his eyes open and smiled at everyone when he saw me and immediately fell asleep. So, me and my surgeon's hands went to work on my friend's intestines in a vodka haze.

Three hours later, I emerged from the O.R. not remembering a single thing I did. I was confident that I had done a competent job but also terrified. I never looked drunk yet I stayed that way until my friend had recovered from the surgery. The first thing he told me was, that as soon as he felt my hands moving inside him, he knew all would be well and I broke down right there while checking his I.V. bag. What the hell! What's a few tears between friends! Then, he took my fingers in his hands and asked where they came from. And right at that moment, his I.V. bag spoke a language of its own, as if it were the birth place of fingers."

Patient In My Own Hospital

"Once I went on a binge for three days and disappeared, like smoke does after awhile. Ended up in a small town and I hadn't washed or changed clothes for a considerable period of time. A doctor in the town discovered who I was and had me airlifted to Calgary. Had to be admitted into the same hospital where I worked as the Chief Surgeon. At first nobody knew what to do with me but a physician friend insisted that I was incapable of treating myself. Then, in the middle of the night, they wheeled me to a private room in a far corner of the hospital. I was so drunk, I kept calling for Room Service, asking anyone to send me up a new head and to please leave the rest of my body alone. And for the next few days, I heard nurse after nurse asking why I couldn't treat myself for my illness. At least somebody there recognized it as an illness because I couldn't. Orderlies walked into my room, saw me and immediately walked out, as if what I had was highly contagious. Some nurses went out of their way to be kind. A few nurses kept looking downward or smoothing out some non-existent wrinkles in their uniforms. Finally, I was told the hospital would explore ways to find me a new head but I first had to admit something."

Headbrace Man

"I've had this headbrace on for four months and it comes off tomorrow. Drove into the same wall three times. The third time did it. Just drank myself out of a job. The usual. Too much vodka in my coffee thermos one day. Always figured that vodka smelled the least and if it did give off a smell, the coffee would cover it up for the most part. But the boss had a real nose for what I was up to. Doctors had to screw this brace to my head and neck.Used a real tool kit, I swear. Felt like I was sleeping in a helmet. Couldn't look both ways when crossing a street so I had to turn my entire body to look left or right. Whenever I stretched, I felt the screws pulling, pulling and it seemed like someone was trying to withdraw my bone marrow the hard way. You should see how I have to shave. Imagine, I'll be able to take a shower for the first time in months. My skin will be in shock. Might wash away much more than the sweat and the dirt. The clean smell will kill me and my sober head won't know what to do and I'll have to pray the marble off statues..

The longest journey for me has been from my head to my heart and to not return."

Unsound

"A Fuller brush Man showed up at my door and said he needed to see me about something other than brushes. Said he's seen me at a bookstore in the mall but didn't get a chance to say hello. I knew it wasn't true and told him so. Next, he said he thought he recognized me as a man with an unsound mind and he knew what an unsound mind was because he sometimes still has one. No, I didn't believe him. Then the truth came out. Apparently, a policeman who had stopped me twice for impaired driving, had suggested that I might need help, that my mind could be unsound too, and he gave him my address.

Well, the Fuller brush Man became my friend. Kept saying he was glad he come along when he did because my mind was sounding like his used to sound every day. Insanity. Doing the same things over and over and expecting different results. Insanity. Like touching the same live wire each day convinced I won't get shocked but still doing it anyway. My brain became more unsounder by the hour. The sounds of my thinking. The sounds of a stranger.

Brushes sound good to me."

Three Wishes

"There I was sitting in a rocking chair on my front porch, my cat nestled in my lap and my brain tied up in booze knots. What I really needed was three wishes and suddenly, POOF! A genie appeared right in front of me on the porch step. I told her that my first wish would be for a golden rocking chair so I could be rich. POOF! My rocking chair instantly turned to gold. Secondly, I wanted to change from being a sixty-six-year-old bag to a young, sexy princess. POOF! Done. There I was a gorgeous young babe in a golden rocking chair. Even my pet cat snuggled closer to me. Finally, I told the genie that my third wish was to turn my cat into a handsome, young, stud of a prince. POOF! Done. There in front of me stood the most sexy young prince, a horny young princess like me could ever want. But then the young prince leaned over and I thought he was going to maybe shove his tongue straight down my throat. Instead, he whispered that I probably now regret having my cat neutered."

Liver And The Noise

"My doctor told me I had a year and a half to live. If I didn't stop drinking my liver would grow to the size of a football and they'd soon have to throw dirt on me. I had no choice. Had one last job offer out there and that was driving a school bus. So I joined a Don't Drink group and stopped drinking. Got me a new hearing aid too, thinking I'd listen better at D.D. meetings. Then, I married a few months later to a woman in D.D. who was twenty-five years younger than me.God, she's a beauty! And I got that job driving a bus load of twelve-to-fifteen year olds twice a day. However, I'd turn down my new hearing aid whenever I went to work and be grateful that I was alive in all the noise. That was sixteen years ago. And my liver, well, I haven't felt it in years. I've also taken up gardening and I turn up my hearing aids so I can hear the worms."

Tell Me My Time

"In my hospital bed, I'm told by the doctor that he can almost count the hours I have left and I wish I could hear my clock ticking as well as my doctor can. Maybe a few days or a couple of weeks. My drinking has burned away too many brain cells. Frying pans of life. For some reason, I don't get the idea of a few days or a couple of weeks. Time has left me. I can't even read the time on my wristwatch anymore. My watch has become a two-legged spider. I hold up my wrist to visitors and beg them to tell me the time. And always they say not to worry, that I have plenty left. Seems that the doctor left instructions for each of my visitors not to tell me the exact time so I wouldn't start counting. I hear excuses such as: forgotten glasses, watches are a waste, broken watches and time shouldn't be measured. To this day, I still don't know the real medical reason why I wasn't told the time by anyone. Or maybe I simply can't remember. All this happened more than two years ago and I'm still alive. And for nearly two years now I have not worn my wristwatch because I don't like that strapped-on feeling anyway. I'm starting to believe that I will live longer if time is out of sight. Clocks wouldn't last a second in my house anyway. My doctor says the heartbeat is more accurate anyway so I'll start counting my heart seconds till I run out of numbers.

In my hospital bed, I'm told by the doctor that he can almost count the hours I have left."

First Frost On My Branches

"This is how I feel after my first drink. I am like the branches of a young tree, frost clinging, freezing me in that precise moment when I stopped worrying and became someone else. The rum self. The frost is always white rum, innocent. I just happen to be in the wrong place at the wrong time, naked, there in the stark winter air. Frozen in my skin shoes. Frozen in the only self I care about. When I reach up to the sky, I know no limits and the arms of clouds welcome me. I charm everyone around me into the same frozen state. Drunk in the frozen breathing. Icicle lungs. Ice man. Every other tree around me is crooked with death. Every other tree bends this way and that, motionless, wondering what I will do next.

If ever I sober up, I promise to be a quiet tree of death licking at the ice of my heart."

Brushcuts And Learning

"See this short brushcut of mine? It's because I want to have as little hair as possible on my head. Want it to look like I just got a haircut yesterday, that it's starting fresh on my head, just like I'm doing in this Don't Drink program.

When I wake up each day, I ask my Greater Spirit, with complete abandon, to show me what I'm supposed to learn today. Protection and care are what I need. I always get some kind of answer, as long as I keep me and my thinking out of the way. Sometimes right away. Sometimes during the day. Sometimes through someone else. If I keep asking what I need to learn, the pressure's off me to try to figure everything out. Try to stay out of my head 'cause that's the worst place to be. Like a prison camp. I just do what I'm told and it works. And then I rub the top of my head in sheer gratitude so my brain remembers who's running the show.

Can you hear the other barbershop sounds?"

The Child Doll

"I like making fun of those dolls that are sold everywhere andI wish I could kill them all. Maybe then some of them would learn to appreciate life. Even as a little girl, I felt that way. Dolls never showed me how to become a person.

Speaking of toy dolls, I used to keep my bottles of booze buried among my flowers. I'd cut out pictures of toy dolls from the Eaton's Catalogue, staple each picture to a popsicle stick and plant the stick right over where the bottle was buried to help me find it later.

My first husband would ask me why I couldn't be just the darling doll in the house instead of spending all that time outside in the garden. He wanted a mother during the day and a whore at night. Each time I came in from my garden, I'd either want to rip my husband's face off, love him to death, or start preaching about the life and death of dolls. Think I drove that man crazy because sometimes the markers for my bottles would disappear because of cats or squirrels. I'd keep digging into the earth because I hated waste and my garden would look like a maze of potholes.

One day, I let my husband in on my bottle-burying secret and he actually said he'd help me find my one or two lost bottles. Instead, he broke them with his shovel and pretended it was an accident. I can just imagine how those few flowers felt. The broken glass. The vodka soil. I was so angry at my husband that right then and there, I decided to divorce him as soon as I could —especially when he joked that I would eventually die as a vodka weed growing in a glass garden.

I like making fun of those dolls that are sold everywhere but I wish I could kill them all."

Have Her Committed

"My cousin who has an ego as big as his waist size, says I look tired and that my face is sagging, like tired rubber that had been left out in the sun too long. Both he and my wife tell me I might want to go see a psychiatrist about my drinking.

So I go to a psychiatrist and tell her how my wife is messing up my life and that I want her committed to a funny farm. But the psychiatrist reminds me that all I had to do is to start attending Don't Drink meetings. No way. I don't have a problem with booze!

I go to a second psychiatrist and tell him how my wife is making my life miserable, that she should be committed to a funny farm. And he too says that I should attend Don't Drink meetings. Sounds like the first shrink called the second one to warn him I was coming. All I want is to get my wife out of the way so I can go on my merry own way and drink my ass off. I keep drinking. And drinking. But the Don't Drink meeting idea is planted and I stop looking to psychiatrists for answers. Meanwhile, my wife doesn't have to mess up my life anymore because I'm doing a fine enough job on my own. However, my index finger keeps pointing at her whenever I think about myself too much.

I am tired. I am ready."

Ears And Mouth

"When I first joined Don't Drink, they told me that my ears need-ed to be fixed first and foremost. They were right. I remember sit-ting in bars and shouting a conversation across the table, across those microphones of beer. My arms and hands would be slicing through the smoke, fists pounding on the table causing only beer glasses to tremble, trying to make a point so I could be right one more time. The music was always loud when I think about it, but not too loud to carry on a shouting conversation, which I consid-ered normal. I discovered that it was my ears that didn't work well. And they got worse. At parties, the more everyone drank, the louder the conversation got — even with the music turned down. Occasionally, I'd find that I was actually screaming at the person beside me when the music volume was suddenly low-ered. Took me a few years before I learned to listen again at Don't Drink meetings. It's true, the ears always go first. Then, the mouth, always the mouth."

Love As A Bonus

"See these tears? They're free.

Should have seen me when I was drinking. When I was gulping rye, I cried rye tears. Sometimes whiskey tears. The world owed me everything. Everyone was against me. Then more rye tears. When I sipped scotch, I cried scotch tears and I was smarter than anyone. Had all the answers. Beat anyone at chess. In my mind anyhow. When I swallowed Southern Comfort, I cried Southern Comfort tears. And I got nasty, mostly because I was afraid of everyone. My mean words could shave off the bottoms of anyone's feet-never mind pulling the carpet out from under them. When I guzzled beer, I cried beer tears. Lots of them. I was the funniest guy in the world. I knew every joke. Every put-down. Every quick come-back. Then I got into D.D and discovered my father had been a member for three years but never told me. My brother joined a year after I did. The three of us laughed new tears. A strange, new joy. We laughed so loudly at our old selves that our faces were exhausted afterwards. Love came as a bonus. Imagine... getting a bonus because of 'once-upon-a-time poor me' tears. Imagine all that me.

See these tears? They're free."

Shocks

"They put me in the hospital for shock treatment. Five kinds of medication were tried and none worked. Then electric shocks were used. Hard to believe but this was the Spring of 1997 and electric shocks were still being used for depression. I was told that it would take some time for my memory to completely return after the shock therapy and that I'll be a little shaky for awhile.

Well, it's six months later and I'm still depressed, still shaky. Not sure if my skin wants to stay on my bones some days. My mood swings have lives of their own. Listen. You can tell by my laughter. Quick, say something funny. Make me laugh. Oh, yea. The one about the pickle in your pocket or are you just glad to see me? Heard that line in an old movie but it's still a good one. Ha! Ha! Ha! Makes me bulge with laughter. My turn. Did you hear the one about the Kindergarten teacher who temporarily lost one of her students named Michael Rotch on a field trip? For an hour, she wandered around asking everyone where Mike Rotch was.

Can you tell? Can you tell by my laugh? People say it sounds like a squeaky outdoor clothesline. Did you hear it? Did you? I figure too many people want to laugh at my laughing but are afraid to. Are you? Are you? What do you mean by 'too many clothes on my clothesline?'"

Met This Woman

"Met this woman a little more than a month ago and she makes my eyebrows turn into one long arc of black hair. My brother says I've dropped ten years off my age. And we're getting married in four months. Can you believe that? We're so crazy about each other that people say we should stitch our grins together. Friends in Don't Drink say my eyes have doubled in size from a month ago. Others say they never realized how tall I was recently and these are people I've known for many years. And she's so, so beautiful, my stomach flips just a little whenever I'm near her. I know it's not infatuation because it is like a friendship that has caught fire; it has taken root and is growing one day at a time. I trust her and have no nagging doubts. We are quiet with each other and laugh at our imperfections. I am warmed by her, even when she is away. Whenever I think of her another sun grows inside me, or a new star warms up a nighttime February sky. When we have sex, all I think about is pleasing her and nothing else; she does the same with me so you can imagine what it's like in bed. I feel like I don't exist unless I can actually feel, smell and taste her skin. When she's not near me, I use the memory of her skin. She lifts me up. Makes me look up. We met at a D.D. meeting and they say that recovering alcoholics fall in love very easily and quite often too. So what? We're different."

Party After Party

"I started drinking at eight years of age. Saw everyone always having a good time, party after party at my house. Saw family members change after a few drinks. Talk more. Talk faster. Louder. Especially my mother who drank her toes off and told the world about a rich boyfriend she used to have, using her high-heel shoe as a microphone.

One time my uncle asked if I'd like to try a shot of rye and ginger ale. Just a shot. I hated the bitter taste at first but my head spun around just enough to help me forget the pukey smell. My uncle laughed and let me take another sip. My head spun a little faster. I loved it. Perfect spinning inside a kid's head. I didn't have to pretend. Didn't get a third sip but I knew right then and there that I loved booze. In fact, during the party, I snuck sips from other glasses. Didn't matter what it was: vodka, rye, rum, sherry, beer, gin. Lots of gin. Finally, I fell asleep on the pile of coats heaped on my bed and hung on to my pillow, as if it were filled with tiny teddy bears.

Later, as people left, I could faintly hear each of them telling my parents how lucky they were to have a child who slept so deeply in the middle of a loud party.

Outside, I heard a freight train click-clacking me into a troubled sleep."

The Silver Bike Idea

"One time, I wanted this silver bike so so badly, that I wouldn't leave the store, even after my parents just left me there whining at the salesman. No, I would not leave that silver bike at any cost. My parents and the salesman tried bribing me, threatening me and finally, physically lifting me up and carrying me out. Even then, I hung onto the bike and caused all kind of toys to be knocked over in the aisles, like bowling pins. My parents turned around and brought me back to the store. Then they left me there with the bike. Told the salesman that he could sell me with the silver bike. I stayed there with the silver bike for an entire afternoon. I wouldn't allow any kid near the bike. The salesman told customers that his bikes did that to children.

All my life I was told to develop a strong will and if I wanted something, to go get it. Demand it if need be. Now that I've spent the last twenty years sober and no more time near any silver bikes, I've had to learn how to give my will away to a Greater Spirit and it was like giving away my insides. Took awhile. Had to unlearn the silver bike idea and stop running the show. Had to unlearn the stomping, the kicking, the crying, the punching by being brought to my knees. Then I had to insist on throwing me away so I could get me back, as if 'away' were a shiny boomerang being flung at the sun."

There I Was In Mexico City

"There I was in Mexico City with two buddies and we're getting drunk in a bar that was so sleazy that even the flies seemed to think twice before flying in the open door and windows. Turns out the place was a whorehouse too. So we all got set up with women and headed to the bedrooms. The woman I was with wanted far more money than I had. Everything up front. Before we did anything. The more often I said we had agreed on one price, the more she increased her fee. Impossible. Impossible passion. Said she was a Mexican feminist. Used the money she made to help promote women's issues, which were many in Mexico City. I told her I was short of her price and she said she'd have me beat up and my photograph printed on one of her feminist posters. She got angrier and angrier and made a quick call downstairs. There was a banging at the door that sounded like sledgehammers. The door flew open and nearly ripped off the hinges. Soon, two wall-sized Mexican men were grabbing me under my arms and lifting me into the air. Then, they flung me out the second-story window, like a white-skinned rag. My clothes were tied into knots and tossed at me, like clumps of clothes fists. Then my emptied wallet was dropped into a bowl of water and dumped on me. When I looked up, I saw the woman taking pictures of the white, white me on the burning sidewalk while the flies became tiny vultures applauding the woman with their wings.

There I was in Mexico City."

Red Underwear

"I was out of my mind on Southern Comfort one rainy night when I decided to run outside in my red long john's. A neighbor called the cops and I vaguely remember being shoved into the back seat of a police cruiser, my red underwear sticking to me like blood-wet cardboard. They took me downtown and I spent the night in a cell that smelled of pee, vomit and sweat. The two other drunks there kept telling me I looked like a giant Christmas decoration and they kept grabbing at me, as if they were looking for an extension cord to plug me in somewhere. My kid brother bailed me out in the morning because my wife refused.

Three days later, I appeared in court and the judge asked me in a loud voice what I was doing out in the pouring rain in my red long john's screaming at the stars and I told him I thought the sky was staring at me for far too long, as if I were in a crowded tavern and everyone there was trying to eye me down. The judge's response was that I'd better get myself and my other body parts to a D.D. meeting as soon as possible so I can learn how the sky doesn't revolve around me and the stars have a world of their own."

Had It All But Death

"I had it all. Cars. Big house. Cottage by a lake. Husband who adored me. Loved my kids. I used to wake up and check the gallon jug of white wine on the night table. See that it was half-empty and this shocked me. I wanted a way to die. Just die. I used to practice dying by pretending to kill my kids as I smoked in bed. I'd get up, tiptoe into their bedrooms and light their bed sheets with my cigarette. Pray. Hope they burned fast. Little pain. After, I'd head back to my bedroom and practice dying by pouring just enough white wine into me to replace my blood. Listen to my children screaming through the flames, wondering, always wondering, why their nightmares have come true. Imagine all that white wine flowing through my veins to my heart and then away again, through my arteries and back to my extremities. If I kept drinking, I wouldn't have to pretend anymore. Drunk toes, feet, legs, arms, hands, fingers. Drunk body parts. Alcohol spilling from my ears.

Earlier today, I caught my husband crying into the morning sun and his fingers gripped his face, like chains."

Drinking In The Can

"I started skipping classes and drinking vodka in the school bathroom. Nobody knew. At least I thought nobody knew. But in chemistry class one day, I poured some vodka into a beaker and pretended that it was a magic potion needing to be drunk right then and there. The chemistry teacher didn't find me so magical and kicked me out of the lab. My father was the principal of the school and he was so embarrassed, he locked me in his office closet. Told his secretary he didn't want to be bothered for the rest of the day. Told me behind the door that I belonged in a locked closet. After an hour, I was just dying for a shot of vodka. My father waited until everyone, including the caretaker had gone home. He let me out of the closet and drove me home, threatening to throw me into the trunk if I opened my mouth.

Two weeks later, I drank myself straight out of home and school into an abandoned apartment building. I pretended I was the only teacher in the best school in the world. And no principal. Never did read another book again and I stuffed my father into an empty vodka bottle, like a kid's transparent toy. You should have seen his face. You should have heard my laughter when I poured him down the drain."

You Know What A Fish Is

"As soon as they threw me into the slammer, I learned what a fish was. Those other inmates were all looking me up and down, like sharks. What could they do to me? What would they get out of me? Then they pretended to kiss me through the bars of their cells as I walked by them. Fingers fantasizing, digging into me. Bellies pressed hard against the bars. Whistles. More smooching. Fortunately, I started going to Don't Drink meetings in the Joint just last week. Never knew that spirituality could make me so tough, so calm. Used to think I was strong before but all I was doing was pretending to be Clint Eastwood. Everyone I met made my day lousy. Funny how those D.D. meetings made my fists feel different. For once, I didn't want or need to show every guy I met how to wear his ribs for earrings. I still feel that way so these morons can kiss me, grab me all they like… only through the bars of their cells. Screw 'em! They don't exist because I will not be their fish and I cannot control how they feel. Let 'em go play in their own aquariums."

Friends

"I was working at this jazz festival when I met this drop dead beautiful woman. Long hair flowing like wheat. Eyes, the color of shiny raisins. A mouth that made my skin tingle. Just thinking of the rest of her made me catch my breath and let it out as slowly as possible. She was an accountant with Imperial Oil. Really intelligent. Great sense of humor, or so I thought. Told her I volunteered as an Uncle-At-Large thinking this would win her over. You know, show her that I'm a sensitive, caring guy of the nineties. It worked and I took her home that night. Just as we were getting really cosy with each other on the couch, the doorbell rang. It was three a.m. Two buddies of mine and a Native woman were drunk as can be. They had met in some classy bar, as you can well imagine. The Native woman pretended she was a barking dog as one of my buddies chased her around my coffee table. Both of them were on their hands and knees. My other friend was almost yelling into my stereo speaker as Three Dog Night sang Joy To The World. That poor accountant couldn't believe that I hung out with such people and left. Suddenly, she had that kind of face that was rehearsing calmness but the veins on her temples became tiny blue water pipes ready to burst east and west of her head.

The next day, she phoned and asked if I'd like some lessons on how to meet real friends and I told her I was too busy practicing my clarinet for the jazz festival tonight. Then she filled my ear with one, long 'too bad'.

That night I played my clarinet with enough joy to light up the sky."

Is It Midnight Yet?

"Is it Friday yet?

I come from Latvia, between the the Baltic and the Black Seas. I was trained to be a radio man so please remember that English is my fourth language. There is lots of silence between my words. I just had what you call a stroke last year and it looks like the right side of my body no longer belongs to me. And I have forgotten the days of the week. Back in Latvia, it was very easy for me to pick up a bottle of whiskey for my father on the way home from school. Not like here.

I got older and my family moved to Calgary. I found it, how you say, confusing, that you had to be twenty-one to buy whiskey here. In Latvia, it was like going to a 7-Eleven store here to buy milk.

All those years, I worked in a radio and later TV repair shop. Then I got my own business. Next door to my shop lived a barber who always brought a bottle of whiskey when he came to visit. After that, the grocery store man on the other side of my shop would see the bottle being opened and come join us for a drink. I don't know how we got all our work done. Don't know how I fixed all the radios and TV's. Nobody ever complained except one woman who wanted to know why the speaker in her radio smelled like whiskey for days.

Is it Friday yet? "

With A Cold Cold Sweat

"Been dry now for about fifteen years. Used to be a biker. Think I killed about four men when I was drinking. Probably beat up at least thirty more who I don't remember. Never got caught for any of the killings. When I went to jail for that last guy I beat up, the judge looked me straight in the eye and ordered me to go to Don't Drink meetings in jail, which I did right away. Figured I'd been beaten to my knees anyway. There was no more bottom to my bottom. And when I got out on parole, I continued going to D.D. meetings.

On my second week out, I met the same judge at a D.D. meeting. Couldn't believe it. Neither could the judge. I was surprised that he remembered me. At first, both of us pretended to be strangers to one another but that didn't last long. Integrity instead of individuality was what I had to remember. When the meeting was over, the judge came over to me and asked how I was. I did the same. Told him there were no hard feelings, that I would have thrown him into the slammer too. And I swear, right then and there, he hugged me with a cold, cold sweat on his face that brought the biker feelings right back to my neck, my spine."

Women Walls

"I don't know what to do with women yet I can't do without them. Go figure. I've been dry for a long time but I'm still learning how to live. My wife plays mind games because I'm not as controllable as when I was boozing. When I was drinking, my behavior was somewhat predictable for her. She knew which bar I drank in. She knew exactly at which point I was getting drunk at parties. Sometimes, she'd even leave the car running when we went to visit someone because she knew it wouldn't take me long to get blasted and I'd have to be driven home. She knew. She knew.

Last Saturday when she wanted me to paint our daughter's bedroom. Instead of asking me straight out to do the job, she kept wondering aloud if I thought the walls looked faded, or my daughter's furniture deserved better-looking walls, or the walls don't look so good with the new carpet, or it looks like the sun has faded the paint. Never once did she ask if I would paint the bedroom walls. Straight out. Just like that. You know, nothing fancy, no games. Maybe, women find answers by just talking out a problem and guys just want an answer. Maybe, I just hate games in sobriety because I used to make up a new one every time I got drunk and opened my mouth to breathe."

Recovering Catholics

"I can't believe the number of Don't Drink people I've met who are also Catholics. Every one of them was brought up with the idea that God was a punishing force only. You sin if you breathe.You sin if you think. You sin if you don't think. You sin if you touch. You sin if you want. You sin if you need. You sin if you feel. Was there any real loving anywhere? I'm beginning to believe that D.D. is also a place for recovering Catholics. Forget the booze. I don't blame God for all of this. After all, He's a Greater Spirit that any religion can call on for help. Maybe, those Catholics never learned that they could only win by giving up. All of them believing, believing, because they're afraid to go to some kind of hell. And all of this believing has taken God away from them. When they go home tonight and get on their knees, I hope they pray for more brains. God brains."

Toilet Paper Bottom

"When I hit my last bottom, I landed on something that felt hard. Rock hard.

Well, I found out soon enough that bottom was really made of tissue paper. Wet tissue paper. Since I've been dry, I've fallen through more bottoms, more hells, but somehow, some way, because of D.D., I don't drink. Perhaps, I'm only given as much tissue paper as I can handle at one time, as if I live just above a toilet paper bottom.

One of these bottoms was when my wife left me after twenty-eight years and I was sober for quite awhile. She said that when I was drinking, I was a drunk baby. Now I am a sober baby and she can't control me anymore. My wife was born to control. Another bottom was when I got fired from my job after twenty-one years with the same company. Same reason, because in the office, I wanted things done my way or the highway. But I guess life ain't easy for anyone whose biggest bottom was when he found out he had to grow up and learn how to change his own diaper. And my wife became terrified when the diapers disappeared. So did my boss.

When I hit my last bottom, I landed on something that felt hard. Rock hard."

Stock Clerk

"It all started one day when I was working at Eaton's as a stock clerk. On the floor, I found a hundred dollar bill, a quarter and a nickel. I returned the nickel only to Lost and Found. I felt brave. Really brave. Then, after work, I was invited to the bar with some of the guys and we sat at a table with members of a motorcycle gang for some reason or other, probably because I thought I was still brave or something. That was it. I watched. I listened. I drank myself stupid. Got tougher. Braver. More mouthy. Began to see all these motorcycle guys behind bars, their leather squishing against the metal. Right at that moment, I could not understand how I never became a crook or gangster. But I never did. I was better than those baboons. So far. Still, there's something about jails I find very curious. Almost like a Lost and Found Department.

Yesterday, my wife told me that I've always been behind bars. I assumed she meant my job but she had more to say on the matter."

They Call Her Red

"Whenever you see my neck getting really saggy, it's because I'm warming up to cry.

Here I am, supposedly a good Catholic woman and I find out I'm pregnant. I had no choice. Had to have it done. I was alone. Unmarried. Drinking my pants off. Screwing my brains out. Used to wear my favorite high-heels when I drank. Called them my I.W.S. shoes, my 'I Want Sex' shoes. So I did it. I went for an abortion. All this happened years ago when you had to go up the back stairs of a doctor's office. Helluva time! I still cry today for taking that child's life. When I have those crying days, I feel the bottom of that hole inside me and I hear a child's voice bouncing off the fleshy walls of my uterus, asking me to keep it alive for the rest of my life. The voice is clear, insistent and it has never left me after all these years. Guilt is hearing a child singing live.

Did I ever tell you that my big brother is a Catholic priest and he too goes to Don't Drink meetings? I used to look up to him and his theology of dying. Now, I call him Saint Sinner and he's just another control freak with his pants down in the wind."

Chin

"I had no chin. None. So I had surgery done. An implant was inserted where my chin should be. After the surgery, the more I drank, the better I thought I looked. I became a movie star in one of those musicals. I think it was called South Pacific. I sang and sang. Loved those lavish musicals. Unfortunately, I had a deep voice because of my smoking. So, I drank more to pretend I had a full range in my voice. I could do it all. In South Pacific, my partner was a dark-haired man who had a very prominent chin and a face you could eat, among other things. He loved my new chin. Said it complemented his own.

One day he asked why I stuck out my chin so much even though I didn't need to anymore. Yes, I could swallow his face and his great voice too but then I choked because his brain was like two I.Q. points that could be rubbed together to make a fire. Too bad he didn't know I had to keep celebrating my new chin. Anyhow, the two of us kept singing in South Pacific and I made sure that my new chin faced the camera at all times, especially after a few drinks. And after a few more shots, I stopped worrying about my leading man and made delicious plans for later."

The Patch

"See this. It's a patch to help me quit smoking. Have to keep wearing it on my upper arm. Good thing I don't have to go to Don't Smoke meetings too. Coming to these Don't Drink meetings takes up lots of my time but I don't care if they take up the rest of my life. But smoking after sex or a good meal... humm...boy, that's going to be tough to do without. Heard another woman say one time that nicotine is like heroine and makes our pores stand up and salute. Here's to a great meal! Here's to sex! I believe her. Maybe, just maybe, I can experiment with this patch. Perhaps, I can take it off with the rest of my clothes before having sex next time and then stick it back on afterwards. See what happens. You never know. You just never know."

Voice

"I used to call her office two or three times a week for machine parts and we'd talk for awhile after the ordering was done. A few weeks passed and I fell in love with the sound of her voice. Found out she's in Don't Drink like me. When we finally met I was knocked out at how beautiful she looked outside too. What a stroke of luck! We fell in love, almost stupidly, and were married within six months. She had two kids and so did I. We put our four kids together in the same house. As I expected, there was conflict. Her kids said I wasn't their father and therefore couldn't tell them what to do. Then my two kids told her she wasn't their mother and couldn't tell them what to do. So nobody told anyone what to do and it was like living on one of those islands with no way off and surrounded by sharks. Well, I watched. I listened. Felt the shark's breathing. Their teeth. Although they fought it, I watched my two sons slowly fall in love with her voice too, like the ending of a 1950's movie. As far as her son and daughter were concerned, well, they just learned to tolerate me, probably by listening to my incessant talking about the love in their mother's voice and why she was teaching me how to talk all over again."

Mexican Cure

"I've been driving trucks for years now and I had to stop. My doctor told me to get my affairs in order because of the cancer in my rectum. I refused to give up and went to the bank instead. Took out all my savings and drove to Mexico where they said they had a magic cure, at least to prolong my life. When I got back after three weeks, I was totally broke but felt better. My doctor was amazed. Colon Cancer. How much longer do I have? Twenty-thousand dollars for a Mexican herbal cure. Has to be more than the conventional cures. Hope this gives me more time. I can already feel my colon stretching from here to Mexico, even after doctors here have removed a huge portion of it. Yesterday, my doctor looked up my rectum and said he could tell me the story of my life. Of course, I thanked him profusely. What's next? I know I don't have to drink booze. Good thing my colon is not attached to my brain. Something must be working. I've now got everything I need and nothing I want and my affairs can take care of themselves."

Trucker's Funeral

"The place is jammed with Don't Drink people – all here to pay their last respects to the trucker in his open coffin. Colon Cancer ate him inside out. Another trucker gives the eulogy and has everyone wiping their eyes: heartfelt man with a generosity the size of a warehouse, used to love his coffee black at Tim Horton's after D.D. meetings. The other trucker chokes, chokes again and cannot finish his words. People are lined up outside too, as if the dead trucker were a celebrity of sorts. But he was not. He was just another recovering drunk in D.D.. If there weren't so many good D.D. people here today and the trucker didn't die sober, there'd only be three people present: two bill collectors and a hit man. The trucker tried so hard to live longer, even after the Cancer had taken over his insides. If he were still drinking before he died, he'd be afraid of death but see no reason to live any longer than necessary. A Mexican miracle cure would never enter his mind and he'd have to imagine his own eulogy strung out in an empty trailer somewhere while thinking of ways for the hearse to carry everything he owns to his grave in a U-Haul."

Woke Up In My Purse

"I was drinking in a tavern with a man on each side of me. I opened my purse and pulled out enough money for one more beer. After awhile I bought a round for the two men. We took turns buying each other beer until I finally convinced both men to come home with me. I was pretty drunk but not totally gone and feeling very horny. So were the two men. Took them back to my house. Took one on at a time in my bedroom. Then they both wanted sex at the same time. I tried but couldn't do it. I was sore everywhere. Really sore. The two men got angry, put on their clothes and emptied my purse before leaving.

Next morning, I awoke with my empty purse over my head, lying naked on my bed and the roof of my mouth felt like the inside of my purse which was not the usual satin. I phoned my gynecologist and she was able to fit me in later on in the afternoon.

At my doctor's office, she took longer than usual for the examination because she said she had to read my insides completely. After the checkup, she told me she'd believe anything I'd say."

Out Again

"Hearing the same drunkalogues from the same people over and over again at the same Don't Drink meetings, was getting to me and my wife. Resentment. Resentment.Then my wife and I did it. One Saturday night we went to a bar and started off with a ginger ale each. After, we switched to beer. The first bottle went down slow and I didn't really enjoy it. Same with the wife. We both tried a second beer and enjoyed the taste even less. Five years of Don't Drink meetings had really screwed up our drinking so we left after two beer each. And the next Saturday, we did the same thing. This time we had three beer each. I hated it. So did my wife. Time to go back to D.D. meetings and we went to one the next morning. It was me. Us. We had forgotten about integrity before individuality and I let me get in the way again. I needed to hear the same stuff over and over because I'm a slow learner. Lucky for me that the doors of D.D. swing both ways. Lucky for me I found out that I couldn't change me or anyone else for that matter. Never drank even ginger ale after that. Stuck to coffee. Black coffee. And water. Clear, cold water."

Pants, Pockets And Rules

"After the D.D. meeting, I asked this stunningly beautiful woman if she'd like to buy a charcoal water filter for her taps and told her that her water would be that much purer, taste that much better. She didn't want or need a water filter. When I asked why she simply said she didn't need to have reasons. Then, I asked if she would like to go for a coffee with me and she flatly refused. Told her that I wouldn't talk about water filters but she still declined. Then she asked me if I had forgotten D.D.'s first rule of behavior and I didn't know what she was talking about. Right away, she told me to keep my wallet in my pocket and that other thing in my pants, so I left her alone right then and there and slipped out the door, stunned by the cold, black air of life without booze."

Ready

"Once I was getting ready to go to a party and I was late, really late. A friend in Don't Drink phoned and asked me to listen to how he felt so bad inside his head because his wife was cheating on him. Depression. I listened. And listened. Finally, he said he felt better and I left for the party. Got there about eleven o'clock and some people were already a little drunk. I recognized the host as the guy my friend's wife was cheating with. In my ear his whiskied breath asked if I had ever had any problems with hemorroids. I told him I was just fine, thank you. Then the host asked everyone to be perfectly quiet and he announced to everyone that he had just met the perfect asshole. Everyone laughed. Even me. After, I whispered in his ear that I couldn't stay too long because I knew he was the guy who was cheating with my friend's wife. But before I leave, I'd like to have just one dance with HIS wife and he froze, like dried blood, there in the middle of the dance floor. They were playing my slow song and I was ready."

I Always Changed

"Whenever I drank, I always changed so fast and just a couple would do it and… My brain squeezed itself dry of all logic. My tongue flapped to itself. With women, I was always shy but when I drank, I became Mr. Hot Shot. I'd be outgoing, charming all the women around me. Mr. Suave. I figured if I could make a woman laugh, I had my hand halfway up her leg. Or so I thought.

One night after four or five beer, I whispered into my friend's sister's ear what I thought was a great joke about a guy who tried to blow up a bus but got his lips burnt on the tail-pipe. After that I slurred that I wanted her to burn her lips on my tail pipe after I took my wife home. Her mouth dropped open and she shoved a bowl of chips into my face. I had chips in my eyes, up my nose, stuck in my mouth, sticking out of my ears. Chips. Chips. Everywhere. Even down my shirt. What a furious woman! Words tripped from my mouth like an ocean of feet and she told me that the only brains I had were between my legs. Then I stood up, bowed and took another couple of swigs of beer - anything to prepare myself for the bowl of pretzels heading my way, like a stainless steel fist of brown nails."

Beer Caps And The Moon

"A man and a woman sit cross-legged, about ten feet directly across from one another on the grass. The stars keep score at this staff party game on a warm June night. As the man drinks his beer, he flips his beer cap at the woman's bottle and tries to knock off her beer cap which is resting upside-down on the neck of her own bottle. The woman does the same to him. Whenever one or the other misses, he or she takes a swig from his or her beer. Whoever knocks off the other's beer cap first, wins a free beer. They play and play but nobody ever wins. Finally, at the end of the party, when nearly everyone has gone home, the man and the woman laugh and tell each other how the sky looks crooked and then fall over their empty beer cases slurring something about the cheating moon, that tricky yellow beer cap in the sky. A man and a woman sit cross-legged."

Drinking Like Us

"I was sipping from a can of Diet Coke at a staff party, minding my own business, when this twerp, who was from Prince Edward Island next to me asked why I wasn't drinking booze, like everybody else. Did I have something to prove to everyone? Was I trying to show that I was better than everyone else? I told him I simply wanted to drink Diet Coke and that's it. I wasn't trying to prove anything to anyone. And no, I wasn't trying to be some kind of pastor or Diet Coke doctor. But he wouldn't let up on me and kept demanding why I wasn't drinking the real stuff. Finally I told him that if I had one drop of alcohol, I become an instant idiot… like him. Well, that did it. He told me to go home to my warm milk and cookies and to come back when I became a real man. Then I got up and I thanked him for all his real man wisdom found in that vast arid region between his ears. The look on his face told me he didn't understand. The look on his face suddenly belonged to a lost boy in a man's suit so I did the right thing and apologized for my own mouthiness."

Vodka And Water

"Do you remember when kids listened to teachers?

A long, long time ago I used to keep two bottles of vodka in my top desk drawer, one empty and one full. The labels of both bottles were peeled off beforehand. I'd start my day leaving the empty vodka bottle on my desk in plain view of everyone. Soon, I'd ask one of my Grade Six students to go fill the bottle with water. Of course, I'd have an empty glass on my desk. After I put my students to work, I'd switch the bottle of water for the bottle of vodka from my drawer. Every day, I'd send a different kid to fill that empty vodka bottle with water. But something started telling me that I was pushing my luck.

One day, I got caught when one of my students, who sat close to the front of the class, was choking on something and just grabbed the glass from my desk. She took a huge swallow of the real vodka and choked even more until I pulled the bottle of water from my drawer. You should have seen the look on that kid's face. The Principal finally learned why I was the happiest teacher on staff, especially just before dismissal when other teachers were grinding their teeth, like pencils in a sharpener.

Do you remember when kids listened to teachers?"

Speaking Of Visions

"I very recently got out of a Detox centre and had to spend a couple of days in a hospital. During that first day in the ward, I woke up after a wonderfully, long nap. Felt like I had spent a month on a warm tropical island. Anyhow, I saw a bright light at the end of my bed. Now, this is all very private to me because I know people won't believe what I'm saying. That vision, that bright light, actually spoke to me. No, it didn't say I was healed or anything like that. The light simply said it would give me the greatest gift of all which was Time, Time to get well. And that time started four years ago and today I am still sober. All this happened on a bright, sunny Saturday afternoon with the sun spreading itself all over me and my room, like a gold quilt. I remember the nurse saying to herself that I must have doubled up on my medication when in actual fact I wasn't on any meds at all. And about that glow at the end of my bed – I don't care if it was normal or not, real or not. I'm at this D.D. meeting aren't I? Clean and sober. Doesn't matter how I got here! And I haven't slept like I do now since I was a boy. Know what I mean?"

Working The Rigs

"Fourteen hour shifts. Eat. Sleep. Shit. Shower. Shave. Eat. Work. And then repeat it all over again. Out in the bush. North of north. Just me and a crew of two men. Drilling. Drilling for oil. Good money though. No family life. Little social life. No life. But every night at eight-thirty, I imagine myself at a Don't Drink meeting. I mouth all the beginning words there in the dark while I'm tightening or loosening something on an oil rig. I pretend to hear each person sharing their drinking and non-drinking lives. Joy. Pain. Relief. Funny. Sad, sad songs. Lying, cheating songs. I tell my own story quietly to the stars, especially the part about hitting a fear bottom so deep, I wanted to jump from a third floor hospital window on a Sunday night. Big deal. Third floor. Ha! And wearing an always-full diaper in an endless puberty existence. I imagine other D.D. people smiling, nodding at my story, telling me silently that it's O.K., it's O.K.. The meeting ends. Men shake my hand. Some grasp me by the shoulders. Women hug me confidently. Time for the meeting after the meeting. The cold, steel rig needs my touch. Again. Stars blink. Promise to protect me from myself. I believe them. I believe them."

One Fifty To Join

"My husband came home from his very first D.D. meeting and we talked and talked until four A.M. about how great the fellowship of Don't Drink was. I was so happy for him but there was something not right about his voice. His voice wanted something from me but I wasn't sure what it was. And just before the sun came up, my husband told me that it cost one hundred and fifty dollars to join D.D. and I found this odd because I thought there were no dues or membership fees in D.D.. But, I was so pleased that he finally discovered a place that would help him with his booze problem that I gave him the money right then and there.Then, we made love like frantic teenagers and I seriously thought we'd explode all over the sheets. Afterwards, he told me he was going out for cigarettes because sex without smoking was like breathing without lungs. That was four months ago and I've haven't seen him since.

My husband and I talked and talked and I was… happy."

Where Can I Go?

"My boss has been so kind. He lets me sleep in his spare bedroom. But everyone drinks in that house. I can't afford to stay there either. I don't want to drink again. Ever. My boss's wife keeps coming on to me and I'm still able to stay clear of her. She makes excuses to come into the spare bedroom, like looking for laundry or checking the furnace vent to make sure I'm warm enough. What could possibly happen to a furnace vent from one day to the next? And can you imagine? Screwing your boss's wife in HIS house.

Three days ago though was too much and I gave into her. She was half in the bag and we had sex on the bathroom sink. Still have a sore knee and a bruised elbow. She said she loved it. Had to keep the cold water running to cool both of us off. The tap mark on her butt looks like a tattoo. This morning at breakfast she asked me if I had washed up yet and her wink was as noticeable as an eclipse of the sun.

I can't look my boss in the eye anymore. I just can't.

Does anyone here tonight know where I can find a safe place to live? I won't mess around with your wife. I won't be any trouble. Promise. I'm learning what's right and what's wrong. Please help me! I'll scrub. I'll polish. I'll even celebrate your floor by sleeping on it."

Plants

"My wife was so angry with me when I moved out but our marriage was over and I was recovering from my boozing. I had changed. She hadn't. Anyhow, I love my flowers and plants, especially the ones I have outside. The front of my house usually looks like a magazine cover. And one day when I was at work, my wife wanted revenge so she dug out everything I had planted and threw it all into the trunk of her car. Must have really thought about what she was doing because she drove to where I worked and dumped all the plants and some soil too, on my car in the parking lot. What a mess! I was really heartbroken. And then I wanted to bury her. I really wanted to bury her in her own garden but she doesn't know a garden from a sidewalk. Instead, I planted three yellow tulips in a small wooden box of soil and placed the box on my deck because I will never have control over people, places or things and I had met this new woman who was born in a garden and she choreographed the slightest change in me."

Up The Aisle Anyway

"Met him in a bar. Where else? He bought me a vodka and tonic. I knew right away I was going to marry this man. One drunk with another drunk. Lots in common. Sure. We drank together quite a bit but I was getting in the way of his boozing and he was interfering with mine. Kinda hard to explain. Guess the booze was twisting us both around so much, it was like we lived in handcuffs. Yea, he started beating me. Mostly punching. First, to the face and head. Then, to other places that wouldn't show as much. Yet, we set a wedding date. Go figure!

On the day of the ceremony, we had a few drinks in the morning and then got dressed. Shortly afterwards, he got angry because I hid his vodka behind the TV. I was in my wedding dress and I figured we should both stop drinking so we looked half-decent for the church. He was furious and pinned me to the floor. The punches kept coming but only in places below my neck so nobody at the wedding would see any bruises. I was too drunk to feel any pain but I remember, yes, I remember quite well, walking up the aisle with him and starting to feel the pain of two cracked ribs but I wouldn't ruin this day for anything."

Mother Blood

"The last time I saw my mother alive was when I first tried on my wedding dress.

I had had a few drinks and my mother's words made me blow up when she told me she was tired of having a drunk for a daughter. That did it! I gulped down the rest of my rum. Smacked her in the face with my empty glass. Grabbed her by her hair and smashed her across the head with my bottle. Next, I pulled her out onto the lawn and kept smacking and punching her head. Suddenly, I realized what I had done but it was too late. Someone had pulled me off her. I was surrounded by neighbors. Paramedics arrived. One of them checked my mother's pulse. She was dead. There were grass stains on my wedding dress and mother blood on my fists. Yes...that... was the last time I saw my mother alive and I kept telling the cops that I wished I could tell her I was sorry.

Years later, I went to visit her grave and spoke my pain, as if my mother's marble ear were the only one listening. By the way, I never did marry. Never could.

The last time I saw my mother was when I first tried on my wedding dress."

Drop By Drop

"When I was in Grade Eight, I loved to be sick. I could stay home from school. After my parents left for work, I got up, got dressed and went downstairs to collect all my father's empty bottles of booze. Then I turned each bottle upside-down and let them stand, each in a booze bottle cap. After, I went upstairs and made myself a peanut butter and grape jelly sandwich. Had a glass of milk and turned on the TV. After three hours of soap operas and quizz shows, I went back downstairs and emptied the last booze drops from each bottle cap. Then, I carefully dripped each bottle cap into one small glass. There were that many leftover drops from each bottle. Amazing how booze can stick to a bottle, especially those liquors, but if you give it time, you'll drink fine. After, I drank that glass slowly and tasted everything from Crème de Menthe to Rum. And that's how really I started drinking. Drop by drop into one glass, as if I were doing a brand new school science experiment."

Electricity

"I knew I was crazy enough but then the thunder and lightning happened and I felt crazier. I was out there, right in the middle of the storm with a drinking buddy. Dark. It was so, so dark we could not see the labels on our booze bottles. We were looking for stars. So, so drunk. Looking for eyes in the sky that could see better than we could. The lightning carved up the black sky and then suddenly ripped it apart. We were terrified. We ducked down to the ground. Back to back. That didn't help much. Stupid. Lightning cracked the sky open again and hit the ground between our backs. The grass beneath our feet was on fire. We took off in opposite directions. I smelled my shirt burning and ripped it off, throwing it at the sky, like a burnt-out, raggedy star.

Didn't hear from my friend until two days later. Thought he was fried to a crisp. When he called, he said he ran away from me because he thought I would set him on fire and asked if I still smelled funny, like he did."

Dogs And The Snowbank

"It was as cold as a witch's boob on Halloween. Stormy too. Had to take my two dogs for a walk in the park. They just had to get out from the cigarette smoke and the stale booze smells. At the park I always had a few bottles of vodka stashed in a snowbank behind a tree. I slipped on my parka, boots, big mitts, tuque and headed out into the blizzard. As I trudged my way through the snow, my dogs looked at me as if they were asking why we were out here in the first place. They knew. They knew. When we got to the park, I dug through a snowdrift and pulled out a twenty-sixer of vodka. Then I just plopped down into the snow and downed nearly half the bottle in two gulps. The snow felt so quiet, so peaceful, like cool feathers melting on my face. Behind some clouds, stars told the story of my life in a code only I understood. Felt like I was sitting in the comfort of my living room, bay-windowed by years of vodka. I took another huge gulp and fell back into the snowbank. Asleep. Dead asleep. Frostbite in my fingers and toes. Nearly frozen pee in my pants. One of the dogs went to get my wife. Good thing. She woke me up with gentle shaking, snow and finally, slaps to the face and I had no idea why I wasn't in my living room anymore."

It's My Sister, You Know

"It's my sister. A real beauty. Inside and out. She's been sober for twelve years. Goes to Don't Drink meetings. Works her recovery well. Reaches out to newcomers. Used to be a hooker on the streets of Vancouver. Made each of her johns wear two condoms. Double rain hats, she called them. Did her best work in the back of a van, she used to say. Now, she's dying of Cancer. Lung Cancer. Tried everything to quit smoking but just couldn't. Hypnosis. The Patch. Nicotine substitutes, like gum. Acupuncture. Reading books. Joining a self-help group. She once said if she were rich like Keith Richards, she'd go to Switzerland, have her blood drained, like the tabloids said, and pay to get new juice pumping through her veins. Even went for a walk through a giant, blackened, rubber lung created by an ex-smoker doctor but all that did was make her throw up. Medical people say it's like she's hooked on heroin and she's got about seven months to live. What can she do? We talk every two days on the phone. She knows she's dying but still tells jokes, like the one about the new national anthem in the White House whose title is: Swallow Your Leader. Says she wants to die in a motel room surrounded by laughing friends while watching old Marx Brothers movies. But my sister doesn't think about drinking. Amazing. And hooking is the last thing on her mind. And she's my sister, you know."

To Do It Properly

"The doctor told me that my face, my skin didn't look too good and that he couldn't keep prescribing Valium. I thought it was because I didn't know how to drink but he said it was because my body was allergic to alcohol and my mind was obsessed by it. I shouldn't be drinking at all. Told me to attend Don't Drink meetings so I could stop drinking altogether. I nodded. Said I agreed with him. But in my head I figured that maybe, just maybe, those Don't Drink groups could teach me how to drink properly. You know, perhaps I could find a meeting where the members all got together to practice their drinking, almost like a Bring Your Own Booze party but without the music. The words inside my head sounded like a tennis ball being hit back and forth. That was all I heard. Even with skin the color of a banana."

Same Man, Same Woman

"I tell ya, she's something else!

After three dates, I loved her, like a man with two hearts, almost as much as my booze. I wanted her like booze. I needed her like booze. She refused to drink along with me. Wanted to leave me and I wanted her for my wife. On our fourth date, she told me we were finished. Walked right out of a party. I was furious. Wanted to kill her. How dare she do that to me! Staggering home on my own, I planned and planned how I'd get her back. Poison. A bomb. Hire a hitman. Run her over on the sidewalk with my car. Name it and I was thinking about it. Got home and fell asleep on top of my clenched fists.

Next day, I awoke with pain in my knuckles and a sore chest. I didn't do anything but pout for the next few days, my bottom lip dragging along the floor, like a baby's blanket. I called D.D. Went to a number of meetings over the next few weeks. Stopped drinking. One day at a time. Met the same woman in the Produce Department at Safeway's. Right next to the apples and oranges. She could not believe I was the same man she once knew. We dated. Got married and to this very day, I'm so grateful that I didn't murder her because it would have killed me if I did.

I tell ya, she's something else!"

Tools

"There we were working on the same contract, same residence. I was painting. He was fixing the plumbing. I just couldn't believe it. What are the odds of this happening? Five years ago, this same guy had stolen some of my tools when we worked on a commercial project together. I knew he was the one but I had to work with him to complete our contract. To get back at him, I painted every one of his own tools a different color with an oil-based paint. The tools he stole from me I left unpainted. Drove him nuts. A green wrench. A white hammer. Purple screwdriver. Yellow pliers. Should have seen his face. The other guys teased him like crazy. Got him good. Then he found out. He knew that I knew he stole some of my tools. But I really couldn't prove it. I owe that guy an amend, yet, I just can't pick up the phone to do it. I know it's part of my recovery in Don't Drink. The amends will have to be done in person. Yea, I'm afraid. I shouldn't worry because I've had to make far bigger amends. Must be those lemon-colored pliers squeezing me. The horn blows for lunch. I get ready to improve my sobriety."

When My Father Said We

"I wanted to ask forgiveness from my dad but he's a retired Irish Catholic cop and I could never do anything good enough for him. School. Sports. My job. My wife. Kids. Anything. Nothing was ever right for him. Finally, he had a massive heart attack and had to be bedridden. The doctors said that his heart was a cement sidewalk with a crack down the middle. The hard heart of my father needed some serious fixing. He had no choice and had to at least consider my request. The next moment was so gentle I could feel leaves falling on the warm lawn inside me. As soon as my father gave up, he won me over. Said he had to talk to me but didn't know how. I told him he could begin with the word 'we' and that he had all the time in the world to learn there in his bed. And we became friends for the first time in forty years, first time since when I was five or six years old when he pretended to be my friend by throwing a baseball back and forth. Behind his fake smile, he either threw too hard or too soft. But right then and there in the hospital, my father let me fluff up his pillow, as if his heart were filled with feathers all along. Then, a nurse came in and gave him a sponge bath. A voice in the ceiling announced the beginning of visiting hours."

Helping

"About a month ago, this guy of about thirty, needed a ride to a D.D. meeting. He was a newcomer, ready to leap out of his shoes at me when he opened his front door. And I could smell a thousand Clorets on his breath. Well, he thought that just because I was driving him to a D.D. meeting, I had a responsibility to give him money too. Right away he asked me for nine dollars so he could do his laundry. Sorry, I told him. No way. I told him I was here to carry the message and not the alcoholic. He didn't like that. Then, in the car, he asked me for cigarette money and I said I didn't have a cent on me which was not true. After, he asked me to help him out with his rent. Even a cheque would do. Told him I didn't have my cheque book with me. Later, he wanted food money. Said he'd wait for me at the ATM machine while I withdrew some dollars for him. He wanted. He wanted. And he expected. Told him that he had to carry himself or he'd pull me down with him and that's the way it is. When we got to the meeting, he lasted about ten minutes then disappeared outside. Seconds after he came back, I could smell the whiskey on his breath and he whispered to me that he'd rather walk home after the meeting."

When I Went Out

"I went out for some bread and milk in St. John's, Newfoundland and ended up in a bar instead.

Four days later I awoke in Toronto to watch the sun rise over a curb. There, lying on the sidewalk, I was so low that a snake's ass looked like a star. I hung onto that curb, my fingers as cold as the cement. Insects walked by my nose and looked like dinosaurs. I listened to high heels clicking by my fingertips. Men, wearing expensive loafers, tiptoed around my throbbing head and fingers, as if they'd seen my hands before, maybe shining their shoes. Kids giggled by in their sneakers. Someone stuffed a five-dollar bill under my shirt collar. Another man moved my body as gently as he could so I wouldn't block pedestrian traffic. A woman tried covering my head with the Sports Page from the Globe And Mail for shelter but decided on a couple of yellow tissues from her purse instead. I should just jump to my feet and blow the last four days away, maybe pretend they never existed on my calendar. But I don't know where those days have gone. Blackout time again. And my wife must still be wondering about the bread and milk so I'll give her a call with my collar money."

In The Early Morning Drugstore

"It was just after Shopper's Drug Mart opened. My wife had asked me to go buy some shampoo and deodorant. I'm standing in line behind this guy and he plunks down six bottles of aftershave lotion on the counter. He's wavering on his feet and the sun streaming through the window makes him look like one of those blow-up dolls that can't sit still in a store window. The clerk takes one look and tells him she can't allow him to buy all that aftershave, that he'll have to put it all back. She knows what he's going to do with all that aftershave. Five minutes later, he returns with enough mouthwash to sweeten the breaths of a dozen mouths — all at the same time. The clerk asks him if he's buying mouthwash for an entire street of mouths and he returns the mouthwash too. The clerk and I waited and waited. The man never returned to the checkout counter, never left the store. The clerk worried. The pharmacist worried. I was amazed at how the man had vanished so quickly. They found the guy later behind some boxes at the end of the cosmetics aisle, with bright blush on his cheeks, purple lipstick all over his mouth and a Lysol can at his lips."

Snow Feet

"It hurts my feet just to walk over there and fill my cup with coffee. Permanent nerve damage to my feet. Doctors say I'll feel the pain for the rest of my life. And it all happened at a Christmas party one night. I was drinking the place dry when at about two a.m., I insisted on going outside to inspect the Christmas lights on the house next door. You know, had to make sure everything was up to snuff. Only thing is I didn't put on any shoes or boots. Twenty below outside. Threw on my jacket and went out into the snow in my stocking feet. Walked next door and started counting, no — actually yelling at, each and every Christmas bulb. By the time I got to a hundred and sixty-one, and having woken up my neighbors, I collapsed into a snowbank and fell asleep. The neighbors just left me there as if I were just another drunken snow angel.

In the morning, I woke up when a folded newspaper clunked me in the face. But my feet weren't working and I couldn't feel a thing. My tongue was a frozen rug. When I tried to get up, I fell right back into the snow, like a big bag of frozen garbage. My feet were not working. Numb. Pain. Had to crawl to my own front door. Rang the door bell with the tip of my frozen newspaper. My wife took in the newspaper and left me there for awhile longer.

I'll feel the pain until the cows come home or I can grow new feet or hell freezes over — whichever comes first."

Christmas Wreath

"I remember that first Christmas when I went to the liquor store and bought all kinds of different booze, in case, just in case visitors came: Crème de Menthe, Southern Comfort, Cherry Brandy, Cognac, Whiskey, Rum, Vodka, Gin. You name it. I bought it. I looked into my shopping cart and lined up the bottles, like a glass Christmas wreath in a shiny, steel cage. Never know who might come over for some Christmas cheer so I'd better have a wide choice. The wreath in my basket got thicker and thicker: Dark red's, Green's, Yellow's, Brown's, White's.

At home, I told my wife that I can create the most amazing Christmas wreath she'll ever see. And then I proceeded to lay out all the bottles on the living-room carpet, like a perfect wreath. And my wreath stayed on the living-room carpet until after supper. Then, I told her that we should keep our new glass wreath exactly where it was for visitors to admire. But nobody showed up that night.

We had a few visitors during Christmas but never enough to even put a dent in my wreath. And one night, I felt that I needed a bright red bottle, like those fire engines, for my wreath. My wife went to bed and I decided to have a few drinks alone. Then, I phoned all kinds of people asking if they knew of any liquor that was fire engine red. Nobody could help me finish my wreath so I decided to drink as much of it as possible. After a couple of hours, my stomach got the better of me and I had to visit that big, white telephone in the bathroom. Flush. Flush. Finally, I saw that red color I was missing when my blood splashed into the toilet bowl. The perfect Christmas wreath floating, swirling, under my red ribboned eyes. Right then and there I sang JOY TO THE WORLD."

At The Cecil Hotel

"Two days after Christmas, we're drinking draft beer in the Cecil Hotel when in walks a wedding party. The bride, a hooker, is dressed in a white gown and the groom in a black tuxedo. Two bridesmaids, also hookers, follow them into the bar. A pimp has just married one of his hookers. Ten minutes later, the groom tells his bride to stand because one of her johns is waiting for her at the door. The bride leaves with her perfect newlywed smile and slips into the hallway. The party continues. In a half-hour, the bride returns with the exact same smile on her face. Leading her over to a corner of the room, the groom sticks out his left hand, twists his wedding band back and forth, cracks his knuckles and then extends his hand. The bride lays six twenty-dollar bills right across his fingers. Returning to the party, like two plastic characters on a wedding cake, the bride and groom smile for more pictures. More hugs. More kisses. And twice more during the evening, the groom points to his new wife and then the hallway, the new bride always returning to place more twenty's in her husband's hand. The wedding reception ends about two a.m. with the groom patting both his jacket pocket and his new wife's backside at the same time as they leave by the back door."

Doors, Owls and Brothers

"My father loved being crazy.

He loved getting drunk because he said it gave him a chance to show how being crazy was important to him. One night, he came home drunk, like he normally did. My mother had locked him out, as per usual. He went around to the back in the freezing winter night and tugged and tugged and banged at the back door. Then he swore so loud that I heard an owl fall out of a tree into a snowbank. I could tell by the sudden end of the owl's song. After, my father yanked the door clean off the door frame. I don't know where he got the strength and he fell back into the snow with the door on top of him, like he was being framed for a snow picture. He pushed the door off him, stood up, wavering like an off-balanced moon, and then trudged into the house. My little brother, who was only a year old at the time, started sobbing from the cold in his crib. Then, the little guy had a seizure. And another. And died while my father was ranting at the light in our empty fridge. Then, I swore I felt that same owl claw my brother's name into the snow before it attacked my father's drunken head.

My father loved being crazy."

Ravens

"I had had enough of my hangovers so I go for a walk in the woods just outside Banff. I notice a couple of ravens carving up clouds, then swooping down into a valley and back up to the clouds directly above me. I watch and watch until one of the birds lands on a tree trunk about thirty feet away from me. For a few seconds, I turn to watch the first raven in the sky who kept swooping up and down and around, over my head, like a huge question mark out of control. And when I check back at the tree stump, the second raven is gone. On the tree stump, a perfectly shaped black feather sits there as delicate as the rib of an angel. Right then and there I finally figure out there had to a Greater Spirit outside of myself, at least for me anyway. Before, the only power I believed in was the face in my bathroom mirror, the same face that didn't know the difference between a raven and a sea gull. The tree bark creaks from the cold."

The Author's First Book

"It was my first book and the owner of the art gallery told me he'd slip a small bottle of Southern Comfort under a pile of my books behind the podium. Use a coffee cup. No one will find out, except those who know I drink about one or two cups of coffee a year. Before I began reading from my new book, I had a little snort. The audience was seated like a big "V."

Outside the big window, was a sex shop across the street. The lights of the sex shop got brighter and brighter, the more sips I took. And the more sips I took, the better I thought I sounded. Yet, the more Southern Comfort I drank, the more nervous I became and the more I read to only one side of the room. The other half of the audience tried to clear throats, or shuffle chairs to make me look their way too but I didn't notice. However, the book launching went well, until afterwards when I had to autograph my book. Drank too much Southern Comfort and I forgot names, easy names. Then I'd fake it by asking if their names had one "t"or two and the snarls on their faces told me that I'd had too much to drink. I was just out of it. Couldn't autograph my way out of a wet paper bag. It was as if my book decided it would now celebrate without me and actually, I wished it luck."

When I Was Twelve

"When I was twelve, I came home drunk for the first time. My mother's voice was furious before she opened her mouth. She sputtered and spat at me and her face scrunched up, like a red shopping bag. With red and white-knuckled fists at her sides, she informed me she'd rather see me dead than drunk. Then she mentioned to me about her hairdressing sister who died from alcohol and the hairdresser's son who also drank too much. After, I heard again about her mouthy brother-in-law, my uncle from California, who was sober for twelve years and then went out drinking again. Mother rage. She hated booze more than I hated authority figures. No mother loving anymore for me.

Every moment after that, I slowly died for her: day by day, week by week, month by month, year by year. I was going to die just for my mother, if that's what it took to get back her loving. When she decided later to throw me out, even before I got my driver's license, my mother insisted that I go die someplace else because there was no way she was going to bury her own son before he buried her.

My mother's voice was furious before she opened her mouth."

Clorets

"Just finished watching Team Canada get beaten by the Russian Red Army Team. Rock, who made a living demolishing buildings, had invited me over for a few beers. We drank   more than any fish ever could. Had very little to eat. Then, I left Rock's place and climbed into my car, like any other day, except today I was drunk and it wasn't even seven p.m. yet. Had to get home to my wife and two young sons. I drove up to a YIELD sign. Looked to my right. Clear. Looked to my left. Couldn't see. Couldn't see oncoming traffic at all. Had to edge my way across because a camper was parked on the corner. Suddenly, WHAM! A guy in a nearly new, gray Olds slammed into me. My door was pushed in but that was it. His Olds was a junk heap. I could have been killed. Right across the street was a grocery store. After the other driver and myself shared our licenses and pink slips, I zipped across the street to the store and bought four packs of Clorets gum. I shoved as many pieces as possible into my mouth and chewed like a mad man before the cops arrived. I must have chewed my face off in the store and then went back to the accident scene. I stepped outside and spat the gum, the size of a golf ball, onto the street. Then, I stuffed only two fresh pieces into my mouth so I wouldn't look suspicious. When the police came to take our statements, the one doing mine had to open all the windows in his vehicle because of the smell. He told me it was a good thing I wasn't being arrested for Clorets' breath.

Should have heard me not talk my way out of that one."

From The Crowbar Hotel

"Woke up in jail so often with the taste of Rum Coolers on my breath that I started calling it the Crowbar Hotel. I always made promises to God that I'd never drink again. Yet, the next day, I'd go out drinking, get drunk and knock over another motorcycle. I don't know why, but I had to knock over somebody's motorcycle. Didn't matter who owned it: a cop, Satan's Choice, Hell's Angels. Even the mayor's motorcycle was one of my targets but don't ask me how I knew. I had to give it just enough of a push to make it fall over. A couple of times I got caught and was smacked around by a biker. Once or twice a cop caught me. Often I'd end up in The Crowbar Hotel. Whenever I got away with knocking over one motorcycle, I'd take off and go looking for another one. By the second or third motorcycle, I'd be tossed into the Crowbar Hotel, charged with disturbing the peace and the pain of punches and kicks were everywhere. Once, after I told a cop about the Rum Coolers, he asked me if that carbonated cough syrup ever did anything for my cold. And I replied that the stuff only helped pay my hotel bills, as if being a smart-ass would guarantee me the best room in the house. I had to beg the cop to take me with him and he agreed on the condition that I book my mouth into a separate hotel."

Hatboxes And Tinsel

"Used to keep my whiskey in my hat boxes on the top shelf. I also hated the sight of any tinsel on our Christmas tree. Made me think that someone was watching me drink from a thousand skinny mirrors. My husband never knew. He checked everywhere for my booze. Said he didn't like the changes inside my head whenever he came home, especially during the Christmas Season. He had everyone watch me, including our kids, neighbors and friends, when I did leave the house. For three weeks one time during December, he hired a private investigator to follow me everywhere. But all I did was go to my closet and try on hat after hat after hat. I'd cover every mirror, except the one in our bathroom, so I could vomit in more privacy when I drank too much. And once every few days, I'd replenish my hatbox supply when I went to the hat store. Made a deal with the store owner and she'd have my "hats" ready. Told everyone, that I was hired at no salary to model hats at home. My head was the perfect size. Now that I'm sober, I hate wearing hats but I use tinsel like crazy at Christmas and I don't care if it's still coming out of the cat's ass in February."

The Watching

"It was Halloween night and I had a party at my place. I promised myself not to drink at all and just watch. See what happens. At the party there were three hula girls and a construction worker. One guy was dressed as a table, complete with paper plates, plastic cup, fork and knife glued to his tablecloth. Then there was Mohammed Ali, a very beautiful woman who had shoe-polished her face and stuffed rolls of toilet paper into the sleeves of her T-shirt to look the part. Next, there was this man dressed like a baby wearing a bonnet and a diaper and drinking beer from a baby bottle hung from his neck with red ribbon. After, there was a Playboy bunny, Ali Baba, a cop, Batman, Wonder Woman, two clowns, a horse, a gypsy, an old lady with a hump on her back that looked like a small bag of potatoes and others I can't remember. There were also three Draculas. I stood behind my bar, sipping straight Diet Pepsi and watching everyone get drunk. Shortly after midnight, I got a call from a neighbor who told me that there were three Dracula's standing at the side of my house having a pee against the same wall. They were too big to be bats so they had to be from my party. Both bathrooms were being used and the three Dracula's had to unload their pee somewhere. But, when I went outside to look and saw the three men in black sighing in the night, I nearly laughed the stars out of the sky because I couldn't take it anymore. I went back inside and broke my promise but figured it was no longer a promise since it was past midnight. Downing five quick beers in succession, I figured I'd had enough of the watching. And the watching had had enough of me."

Pigeon

"I tried to explain to the newcomer.

When he came back to my place for a coffee, I warned him that he had to do everything to stay sober. Told him it's like a pigeon that is hard to train. Can happen to any bird. In fact, I had one pigeon that I had trained and trained to fly to a destination first and then come home. After three unsuccessful attempts, I had to snap the pigeon's neck just a few minutes ago so it wouldn't ever make a mistake again. No sense in trying to wring blood out of stone. Must have had the intelligence of a rock too. All that bird did was fly up into the sky, like it owned the place, make two circles and then fly straight back home. Just like a drunk who keeps going back for more and never learns until he hits some kind of a bottom or his neck is broken. Anyhow, I just threw the dead pigeon into my garbage can where it couldn't misbehave ever again. Then, the newcomer rubbed his own neck, studied me and threw up right on my kitchen floor, his innards looking like shattered coffee cups and lost baby birds.

I tried to explain to the newcomer."

Wine

"I remember when I was about five and my little brother was a few months old. My father was drunk and feeding my baby brother red wine from a baby bottle.

This didn't feel right to me. My father kept telling my brother to stop crying like a little bastard baby. Laughing aloud as my brother choked and spat, my father pretended he was wounded from all the red wine on his shirt. My brother's baby face scrunched up, scared by the bitter taste of wine. I know I was terrified. We certainly didn't want to wound our father. No, we didn't want to hurt him. Then, my father tried to make me drink a tumbler of the red wine and I didn't want anything to do with this blood. Have you ever known any kid who would drink his father's blood? Right! Besides, the taste was awful. He tried to force me but my mouth was so tightly closed and my cheeks made knots on my face. I too spat out the few drops that made it into my mouth. My father cursed my face from top to bottom because my aim was higher than my brother's.

In bed that night, I could still smell the bastard baby in my father's blood."

Oil Lamps And Cracks

"We moved seventeen times by the time I was twelve years old and I used to think that even the moon must be rented from somebody.

Finally, after another fight with another landlord about late rent, we packed up in the middle of the night and moved to an old abandoned house about eight miles outside of town. It was a biting cold, February night. Didn't take us long to get settled but I have to say that I've never lived in such a dump since. Floorboards sprang up everywhere. Broken windows. The place constantly smelled of damp wood, tobacco, an open sewer and whiskey. Hungry rats, the size of cats took over the place at night and they once chewed off that floppy piece of cartilage hanging from the bottom of my infected left ear. They also took a bite or two from that fleshy part between my thumb and forefinger. The only time I felt warm and safe was at school and in stores. When I stood outside the abandoned house at night I could see light from our oil lamps seeping through the cracks. We had no heat, no electricity, no drinking water or toilet. Had to get water from a well. My father always had enough money for his whiskey though and he would tell us that the utilities were in his brown bottle. We stayed in that house longer than any other place we lived in. Must have been a year or so and it felt good to not have to move in the light of a hired moon again."

Wrong Beetle

"Peter and I drive to the pub downtown in my Beetle and I park in an alleyway close by. We go to Toe Blake's Tavern across the street first to have a few drafts and get a cheap buzz before we hit the pub and its more expensive beer. An hour and a half later we run across the street to the pub with that cheap draft beer glow on our faces. We order a beer. Check out the place for available women and there are a few, or so it seems. Bet the women are checking us out too, or so we'd like to think. Almost immediately, Peter connects very well with a redheaded woman after only two dances. Meanwhile, I'm not getting anywhere. I try and try but I think I had too much to drink at Toe Blake's and women inhale deeply when they hear my stupidity. Midnight arrives and Peter wants to leave with the woman he met but has no place to go, if you know what I mean. He borrows the keys to my Beetle and staggers out of the pub with the redhead. They turn the corner, then into an alley where Peter spots a Beetle. Before inserting the key, he tries the door and it's unlocked. Tumbling into the back seat, Peter and the redhead climb all over each other and jeans end up on the steering wheel. The windows get all steamed up. The Beetle rocks and rocks in the alley night. Suddenly, a door opens and it's a man Peter doesn't recognize. The guy wants to know right now how the hell they got into HIS Beetle and all Peter could think of was how he did it all without a key."

The Big Time Stare

"There I was working quietly in my own drugstore.

I was doing Upper's. I was doing Downer's. You name it - like a kid in a candy store. And when I went home, I had my booze stashed behind my pharmaceutical journals. Had to keep up with my professional reading, you know. Through all this I somehow managed to fill prescriptions for dozens of people every day.

One afternoon, a patient gave me her prescription for antibiotics and I gave her birth control pills instead. The woman was fifty-eight years old. Good thing I caught my mistake and fixed it all up. As she was paying though, I fell into a big time stare and she had to call me by name three times. Didn't work. Then, she reached across the counter and tapped me on the shoulder. Still the big stare, back and forth, from the woman to her prescription and back again. After, the woman grabbed another customer close by and he tried to get my attention by gently tossing a box of cough drops at me. Later, another clerk came and went behind the counter. She took charge. Sat me down. Told everyone that the pharmacy was now closed. A short time after, two policemen arrived and led me out of the drugstore to their car. As I lowered myself to get in, I banged my head, even after one of the officers tried to guide me into the car. Immediately after slumping into the back seat, I found myself slipping in that clean smelling, cop car world and the swirling red light on the hood looked like a cough syrup bottle with a life of its own.

There I was working quietly in my own drugstore."

Head boards And Television

"It happened every time my television ran out of programs. You know, late at night and the testing patterns filled the screen. As soon as that black and white Indian came on the screen, I'd cry and cry into my beer, drunk as a skunk. The television had no more to say to me and that made me a very sad drunk. Shortly after, I'd go into my bedroom and collapse on my bed, like a big sack of fertilizer. That's how I saw myself – a huge bag of crap! Halfway through my broken sleep, I'd awake and stand on my bed facing the headboard. Then I'd pee all over my headboard thinking I was in my bathroom. I'd also talk to that deadened television inside my head. Wait forever for commercials. Later, I bought a color television and by that time, programs were on all night- especially those re-runs of re-runs. Had no more excuses to be sad. Can you believe that! I tried to remember where the bathroom was by leaving a pillow and blanket on the bathroom floor. Nothing helped. I kept peeing on my headboard. The only time it stopped was when my television broke down. I stopped crying totally during another re-run of M.A.S.H. – the story when Hawkeye and Trapper wait until Frank Burns is asleep and then let his fingers slip into a glass of warm water. Laughing like hell, I went to bed drunk hoping I wouldn't pee in my bed, like Frank Burns did."

The Manuscript Of My Son's Death

"My son was murdered in Australia and I wasn't there for him because I was on a bender. I flew there after his wife phoned me for the first time in six years. When I got to Sidney, I discovered that the trial finished the day before I arrived and my son's murderer was sentenced to life in the slammer. I went to the actual courtroom where the trial had been held and I thought of the times when I told my son I'd be home for his birthday but never made it because of my drinking. Yes, I know, I know - another cliché sob story. So what! Don't ask me how I did it but I got a copy of the trial transcripts. The courtroom was completely empty except for the sound of my son's voice asking God if he could be alive again just to see me. After, I sat down and read the transcripts and wept and wept for the blow by blow account of how my son's heart was taken away from him, from me. Stabbed by a drunk in a parking lot outside a bar, my boy was killed for forty dollars, my forty-buck son. After, I got to my feet and walked towards the EXIT. The door was locked. I tried another door and it too was locked. I tried another and another until a judge in his black robes unlocked one door and stepped into the courtroom. After I told him I got locked in, he informed me that nothing happens by accident.

Later, I half-stumbled out into the hot Australian day and the sun burnt a second hole in my black heart.

My son was murdered in Australia and I wasn't there for him because I had myself tied to me."

Daughter

"I used to hear my daughter constantly asking me where I had been, what time I got home, who I was with, what was I doing and on and on. Of course, I'd be out somewhere sucking back the booze. Somehow, my daughter would wake up, clean me up and put me to bed. She knew where I'd been, what time I got home, who was I with and what was I doing. But still she would ask anyway. My daughter did all this for what seemed like years. Sometimes, she'd receive a phone call and she'd walk to get me or take a taxi. And always very calm about it all, even when my clothes were splattered in vomit or blood. Reached a point where my doctor would phone my daughter to check up on my drinking. Finally, two months ago, she helped to check me in at the treatment center. Someone there said she sounded like my mother. I forget how old she is now because the booze has killed so many of my brain cells. I think she's fourteen or fifteen. I'll have to ask her. Did I tell you that my wife left me long ago for my daughter's teacher? You know what those preachy teachers are like?"

Ducks, Trucks And Meat

"Me and my buddy were having a few cold ones one afternoon when we decided to go hunting for ducks in a farmer's field. Before leaving we had a few more grenades and then picked up a couple of bottles of whiskey. By the time we got to the farmer's field, we were pretty ripped and started shooting at anything that was flying. After awhile, there was nothing left in the sky except for a few clouds with shotgun holes in them. No kidding, the sky sounded dead. The farmer came out in his pickup truck and reminded us that it was not duck hunting season. We answered him with a few shotgun blasts at his tires. On four very flat tires, the farmer turned the truck around and drove back to his farmhouse. Later, he returned with his own shotgun and blasted a couple over our heads. That did it! Over to our left stood one of his cows and we all took aim at it. But we just couldn't shoot, no matter how drunk we were. Instead, we collapsed right there in the mud, our shotguns feeling like anchors, and woke up the next day in what I thought was an army barracks. With a hangover as big as the farmer's field, I tumbled out of my cot to go to the bathroom. Then, I discovered that the door was made entirely of cold, steel bars. And suddenly, there was the smell of rotting meat everywhere."

Uphill Mother

"I knew I was getting better. I knew.

One day, I had to carry my mother in my arms for the first time ever. She was simply too tired to use her walker going uphill to return to my car. Wheezing, her legs nearly buckled because the incline was too much. We had just visited the Bow River down by Edworthy Park and listened to the water tongues tell us silent stories of a river filled with many other brown bottle lives. My daughter picked up my mother's walker and we headed up the bike path to the parking lot.

I was sober for thirteen years only two days ago and here I was, walking uphill with my mother and feeling grateful too. And in my arms my mother's sour breath whispered into my ear that everyone was watching us, that they might think she was sick or something. I almost dropped her right there because of my laughter. Because of the way she's lived through the last few years without her own booze but without any help from Don't Drink meetings. Because she thinks she's much too tough to admit she has a problem with alcohol and would go ten rounds with anyone to prove it. My mother and I have always been moving uphill on each other. This is the first hill we've climbed together.

I knew I was getting better. I knew."

Train Station

"I was brought up in a train station and we lived on the second floor. As my dad sold train tickets, he slurped vodka and water from a straw in his water bottle. Mom often yelled at him for using so much money to buy booze but he didn't care. Once he told her that he needed his vodka and water to help him sell more train tickets to farther and farther destinations. Said it brought more money in. He'd actually convinced passengers that they should travel further for the scenery and then come back to where they really had to go. Some passengers truly believed him! They thought they'd pay a little more just for the scenery and it gave them more time to enjoy their train ride. Dad had his extra-long straw sticking out of his water bottle and nobody, but nobody, including passengers, ever questioned him. We were never allowed into the wicket when he was selling tickets. Then, one day, my mother had had enough and replaced his vodka with vinegar. You should have seen my father's face. You should have heard him gasping, choking. He actually threw up all over a woman passenger who was dressed in scarlet red from head to toe.

The next day my father checked into a treatment center because he said he wanted to get his stomach back. My mother took over the ticket selling and surprised everyone."

Bootlegging And The Muskrat

"My father pulled me out of Grade Four so I could sell home-made booze to his customers. We actually had a 'still in every room of the house. Imagine having a 'still in your bathroom! We did. If I didn't bring back money to my father, he would punch me with fists that were as big as ham bones. He was six-foot-five and had a temper that scared the cops. I knew nothing but beatings. Sometimes the cops would get a tip and follow me. Somehow, I'd hide out in the woods. Once I hid in a pond of reeds and one of my father's bottles broke when I rolled over onto a rock. A muskrat must have had a few mouthfuls and seemed to want to play with me. A cop spotted the muskrat hopping in and out of the pond and doing flips, so he came down to investigate. I took off so fast that I dropped another bottle of my father's moonshine. Heard the crunching when the cop stepped on the broken glass but I was too fast for him.

To this day, I still wonder about 'stills, muskrats, glass and more glass. And I always move carefully under the nighttime sky because I never know when I'll be hit by another falling, father star."

Mother In Glass

"There's my mother trapped between panes of glass. Look at her! Her mouth is wide open and her eyes are huge on a face as tight as a new leather basketball. If her eyes grow any larger, they'll take over her face. Her eyebrows are arched like thick skid marks. She's trying desperately to escape with all her mother skin. Thick, mother-made fear smudged against glass. Her teeth are begging behind her stretched, inward lips. I hear her whiskey voice telling me for the first time that I'm right and she's wrong. Is that my mother speaking? I always did everything according to the way I thought Mother would want. Thank you for speaking up, Mother! Thank you! Didn't know you had it in you."

First

"I didn't know if I was speaking Spanish or English.

When the plane landed in Mexico City, I was so drunk, the back of my skirt was tucked into my pantyhose and my blouse was open to just below my bra. Must have been the heat in the plane. I was the first one out of my seat and when the plane finally stopped, I shot to the front of the plane, just outside the door to the pilot's cabin. Thump! The cabin door opened and the co-pilot stuck out his head and asked me where I was coming from. Very funny, I said, but I'm dying for a smoke. Told him he was quite comical about this flying business and why didn't he just flock off. Two flight attendants tried to hold me back so a handicapped senior citizen could slide into a wheelchair but I was out the door before anyone. To hell with the old man! Give him some gin for his bad back. Let him rub whiskey over his bad legs. Get someone to massage his spine with cognac. Not my fault he lives in a wheelchair. Screw him! I'm first and that's it! I need a drink!

After I made it to the ramp entrance, I asked the gate agent where I could find the nearest screwdriver so I could tuck in the rest of my skirt.

I didn't know if I was speaking Spanish or English."

Phone

"I drank so much in the services that my commanding officer decided that I needed a brand new, special job for at least a week. My function was to sit by a telephone in a room that had nothing in it except for a telephone, desk and chair. Between five p.m. and one a.m., my duties included sitting by that phone and to wait for phone calls. I had to record any messages. One bathroom and one meal break during my shift was all I was allowed but I had to eat my sandwiches by the phone. Nobody ever entered the room while I was there. Did this for one full week and the phone never rang once. About halfway through my last shift, I picked up the telephone receiver and discovered that the line was dead. Didn't take me long to I figure out why I was never relieved at one o'clock in the morning for my brand new special job. Then, I heard the door behind me slowly creak open."

Sure About Neil

"I was finished with the booze so I checked myself into the hospital that evening. It was amazing how they found a bed for me right away with all the cutbacks and so on. Anyhow, after a few minutes, I heard Neil Diamond singing Song Sung Blue. Made me close my eyes. I kept hearing Song Sung Blue. Neil Diamond's voice was as clear as the sky used to be for me. There was skinny Neil on stage wearing one of those glittery shirts again and his shoulders weren't broad enough to carry all those stones attached to his chest. A nurse gave me a pill to sleep but Neil Diamond would not leave. He moved across the stage and kept singing the same song, even though there was a promise of a next song. Finally, just after midnight, I called for the nurse again and asked her to tell my roommate to please turn off Song Sung Blue so I could sleep. But she told me I had no roommate and there was no Neil Diamond or Song Sung Blue anywhere. Then, I told the nurse that I gave everything away to my daughter in a living will, including all my Neil Diamond music, because I had never seen a coffin filled with records and CDs at a funeral and I was sure Neil would understand."

When I Was A Horse Thief

"Got so blindly drunk one night and stumbled over to the R.C.M.P. detachment just a short distance from my place. I also made sure I brought along a new twenty-sixer of rum with me. A woman like me needs her juice. When I got there, I saw a beautiful, brown mare tied to a post outside the front door. What an animal! I decided to take the horse for a ride. I jumped on. Fell off. Jumped on again. Took off, just me and my rum and my horse. We ran at a gallop for about two or three minutes and suddenly stopped. I took off my hat. Slid off the mare. Poured some rum into my hat and gave the horse a good drink. The mare wanted a second pour and drank nearly half my rum bottle. Falling back on its haunches after awhile, the horse either refused or couldn't get up. I tried everything. Pulling. Pushing. Sweet-talking. Yelling. Mumbling. Suddenly, an R.C.M.P. constable appeared out of the trees and grabbed me by the collar. Told me that there's a law in the books which allows a horse thief to be hung or shot on the spot. Being the drunken smart-ass that I was, I told him I could have him arrested for allowing me to drive a drunken vehicle. Well, he didn't find that so funny and I had to stare at the moon all the way back to make the handcuff pain go away, as if the moon were made of mercy."

The Squeaking

"Every damn night at exactly two a.m., the young couple upstairs go at it. I can hear their bed going up and down, up and down. Squeak! Squeak! Squeak! Squeak! The loud, heavy breathing, the laughter wake me up every time. From their apartment, I can hear the Supremes singing Baby, Baby, Where Did Our Love Go. Can't be that exciting for them because at exactly eight minutes after two, the squeaking stops. Then I get up. Go to the bathroom. Sit on the toilet seat. Wait until I think they are asleep. After, I screw on the cap of my huge, unbreakable bottle of mouthwash very tightly and bounce the bottle off the ceiling for about eight minutes. I breathe heavily and loudly. Make loud squeaking sounds. Sounds travel well in the bathroom, as you all know. I laugh and laugh until I hear them banging on my ceiling.

And this is what resentment can do to a recovering alcoholic at two a.m. This could lead me to drink again because I cannot afford the luxury of anger. Tomorrow, I will leave a note on their door and give myself a sleeping pill by going to a Don't Drink meeting."

Highway Death

"There I was hitchhiking back into the city after working on my recovery in a treatment center. I needed to walk the fresh air into my lungs. As I was moving along the highway shoulder, a German Shepherd dog came running towards me, barking and growling like crazy. The dog didn't seem mad or anything. Looked like it was trying to tell me something but I ignored the beast, just in case it might want to take a bite out of me. Besides, I don't speak German. Soon, the dog came closer and closer and gazed at me, stared across the highway and back to me again, as if it were asking me to follow it across the road. Still I ignored the German Shepherd and kept moving. And when I finally reached the city, I discovered that my girlfriend was buried in a shallow grave along that same highway where I had met the German Shepherd. Sexually assaulted a few times. Butchered to death by an alphabet of rage. Apparently, whoever did it, stabbed her chest so many times, it looked like teeth marks. The time of death was about one hour before I met the German Shepherd. Had the R.C.M.P. at my door for six months after that.

Yesterday, I went for a long walk and the clouds tried to teach me another word for forgiveness."

My Father's Movies

"I grew up in a projection booth. My father ran movies at the old theatre in the East End. Mom left us when I was seven for a lead guitar player in a Rock and Roll band called The Huntsmen who all dressed in the same wine-colored blazers and gray flannel slacks. Mom was crazy about guitar rifts. Every other family around us had a father, a mother and at least two kids. In our apartment, it was just myself and my dad and his job as a movie projectionist. Often, he'd have to take me to work with him and I'd do my homework right there on the projection room floor. Eat free popcorn. Drink free Coke. My father wrapped me in a blanket and I slept right there by his feet if he had to do a late show, which was quite often. Most of the movies my father showed had happy endings. So when I got older, I assumed I had to get married to ensure a happy ending. Unfortunately, I got divorced soon after and I wondered why the relationship wasn't like the ones in my father's projection room. Then I married and divorced again and again. I blamed those idiot men I got stuck with and I hated every last one of them for ruining my father's movies but I stayed sober regardless.

I grew up in a projection booth."

Heart

"It was Christmas and I just spent twenty-six hundred dollars on gifts for my girlfriend and her two kids. I suppose they paid for those gifts too because I was drunk for most of the holiday. Christmas was when I really tied one on. Helped me cover my past with a mattress, so to speak.

Her gift to me were three oversized, white T-shirts. When I woke up on Christmas morning with a hangover that could turn a Christmas tree brown, she told me I was a no good piece of crap and that her comb had more mental agility than I did. My brain was too sore to argue with her.

That afternoon, while I was napping, my girlfriend took off with the gifts and the kids. She left me with one brand new, white T-shirt and took two for herself. At least I had great sex on a regular basis with her and one new T-shirt. Later, when I tried on the T-shirt, I noticed that my ex had cut out a perfect heart shape where my real heart would normally be. I found the cutout, white T-shirt heart stapled to the front of my black leather jacket.

My girlfriend was pure. So, so pure."

Love and Lipstick

"After the first few days of my sobriety, I began wearing long-sleeved blouses, then sweaters and more sweaters. I thought that the more clothes I wore, the more I could keep my feelings from spilling out of me. No kidding! After, I resorted to a ski jacket and last, an oversized, winter coat over that. At a Don't Drink meeting one night, another woman asked me why I was sweating so much and why I was wearing a big winter coat indoors. First, I took off the coat, then the ski jacket, then the sweaters, then the long-sleeved blouses until finally I was down to a bright yellow T-shirt and white shorts. Sweat was just pouring down my body and I began to shiver in the stink of my body odor. I ran to the washroom and dried myself with paper towels. Soon, the feelings just poured out into the bathroom mirror non-stop – dishonesty, fear, resentment and selfishness until finally... finally I wasn't so afraid anymore. For me, fear was another word for breathing. Then, I drew a smile on the mirror with my lipstick and wrote the word 'love' under the bottom lip. When I returned to the meeting, the discussion was over and everyone asked me what I was in the mood for."

Riding The White Horse

"See this combed back hair, red sports jacket, black pants, black cowboy shirt and string tie – well they are all part of my protector's suit. I'm wearing them tonight to show you basically how I look when I ride my white horse and try to protect someone. Protecting has got me into so much trouble, nothing but trouble, especially with women. Today, many women don't need or want to be protected by men. I forget sometimes. I have to remember that when I'm trying to protect, I'm saying to the woman that I'm here to save her, she owes me and when is she going to pay me back. You know, the usual.

Last week, I was at one of those automated bank tellers. Must have been around eleven o'clock at night. A woman beside me had just finished withdrawing cash, when a man in a black toque approached her near her car and demanded her money. I could hear her simply telling the guy to screw off and to go get a job. As she unlocked her car door, the man grabbed her arm and tried to take the cash from her ski jacket pocket. When I offered to help, she also told me to screw off. And then she proceeded to kick her assailant so hard between the legs that he lost his rasping, canary voice on the spot. Then, she climbed into her vehicle, turned around and nudged the folded-over man into a snowbank. Before driving out of the parking lot, she rolled down her window and flung the contents of her ashtray into his face and that was it for me and my protecting."

Spoons, Sinks And Other Variables

"I woke up on Saturday morning and there it was again. I heard that angry spoon clanging in the kitchen sink. Coffee spoon anger. My mother had another hangover. First one spoon, then a second. My father was still drunk from last night. That spoon sound did it. Here I was fourteen and that spoon noise was louder than ever before. Spoon after spoon. Sounded like a thin chain rattling on tin or glass. I packed some clothes and slipped out the back door. It was easier, safer, living on the streets with my new friends. I had tried it before. Thought it was harder on the streets then but anything is easier than this. I'm sure it will be better this time. The streets have few spoons or sinks. No brothers and sisters beating me or stealing change from my jeans or grabbing me where I shouldn't be grabbed. No mother always whining that if it weren't for us crappy kids, she'd be in Hollywood having a life. No father complaining that we keep his pockets empty! Yet, one minute my father is telling me how proud he is of me and then giving me ten bucks to go spend at the Mac's Store. An hour later, he's telling me how useless I am. All I ever want is a free ten-dollar bill to go spend at the Mac's store. And my mother with her arms around me one minute and shortly afterwards, she's almost hissing her Hollywood spit at me.

When I do find a sink in an alley, it's a quiet sink because it has been thrown out. Not like me."

174

Hat And The Queen

"I was in the army mess hall, smelling like I had draft beer dripping from my pores. I just got back to Winnipeg after a two-week leave in Banff. Bought myself a cowboy hat in Calgary on the way back. In the mess hall we weren't allowed to wear hats out of respect for the giant picture of the Queen which hung right above my head. I refused to take off my new cowboy hat. What the hell was so special about a queen from some tight-ass, bankrupt country still thinking it carries political weight? After, our waiter politely asked me to hang up my cowboy hat somewhere. I told him that the only 'somewhere' was on my head. Then, another soldier told me I'd better remove my hat because the Queen may frown from her picture. Think I cared? Why doesn't that old lady just split up her millions of dollars and share it with all those poor English people, especially street people, who don't even own a wall for pictures. Finally, two military policemen came in and dragged me out by the ankles. I still hung on to my cowboy hat though. As I went head over heels down the cement steps, I hung on to my hat. Nothing else mattered. On the street, a car squealed to a sudden stop and I suddenly thought of a wonderful plan to wipe that smirk off the Queen's face."

Fractions Of Sex

"Never could totally figure it out how sex can be measured in fractions, but sex is one-third of my problem. Funny how people hardly ever talk about sex at those booze meetings. Wonder why? We all have sex in our lives. I hope. And last week, I joined a sex support group. Same process as the booze meetings, except the alcohol is replaced with sex. Anyhow, sex is unmanageable for me. At Don't Drink meetings, members just allude to 'checking out that woman or checking out that man'. I figure I don't need to check out sex at all because sex has me by the shorts. I'm trapped. Can't keep my mind off it. I'm especially hooked on cyber sex. Besides looking for possible e-mail, the only reason I turn on my computer is to check out the pornographic web sites. There are chat rooms, excerpts from porno movies and pictures, lots of sexy thumbnail pictures. I usually get up when my wife is asleep and have sex with myself while watching the computer screen. Our own sex life is horrible. The last time we had sex was weeks ago and I was impotent until I began fantasizing about a woman I remembered from my computer. My wife is now rubbing lotion all over her body and I hear her telling herself over and over that she is worth it, she is worth it.

I've thought of asking her to create her own sexy web site. She certainly has the mind and the body for it. Just a month ago, I bought her some sexy underwear but she only wore it once."

Nose

"See this nose of mine? It's been punched so often, I wouldn't know a straight nose if it sneezed in my face. And always it's because of some drunken brawl. First, my nose looked like your normal nose. It might bleed once in awhile from a fight but nothing too serious. Next, I got into three bar fights in a row. Must have had it broken at least once. Afterwards, my nose seemed to spread itself across my face, like an extra cheek or something. I stayed away from bars so it could heal and I was able to breathe a little easier. To celebrate my better breathing, I went out for a few drinks and sure enough, I got into another bar fight and my nose got smacked again. This time it looked and felt so bad that it seemed like someone had stuffed my nose into my face. A blob of flesh belonging on a horror movie face. Broken. Fixed. Broken. Fixed. All because... because I could not give my alcoholic mouth a rest. I've thought of trading in my mouth for a new one but... what would I look like then? Then there's my nose again. I can't get away from it. My face would be safer in a movie because I've seen all the Rocky movies twice."

This Fisting

"It got so bad I had to shake my fist in the air to help me remember what I did when I was drinking. Let me explain. If I borrowed money from someone, I'd take out my wallet, clench my fist and shake both it and my wallet at the ceiling. Somehow, the memory of both fist and wallet working together never left me in my drunken haze. Yet, I always worried about money when I was either drunk or sober. Didn't matter. And if I had to remember something for work the next day, I'd stand and shake my writing hand, my left hand, at the wall closest to me, as if I were writing a reminder list on the wall. Funny, but this fisting helped me remember all kinds of things: doctor's appointments, bringing the car in for an oil change, social engagements and remembering to buy a gift for my daughter's birthday. Then, one night I shook both fists at a window to help me remember I had two plane tickets to Hawaii for tomorrow with my wife. But I drank much more than I ever have and woke up the next day on the mess hall floor. My two fists were bloodied and looked like they belonged to a leper. Standing over me with knuckles clenched in beer- foam anger, was my wife holding our suitcases. When I asked her if we had missed our flight, she kicked one of my fists, as if it were a child's toy blocking her path. Then, I heard soldiers marching.

It got so bad."

The Same

"It was always the same.

I'd have a couple of beer at home and then head to the tavern to drink cheap draft beer with my buddies. I'm sure you've heard this routine before but it worked for me. It was a cheap way to get liquor into my blood and then head over to the clubs to meet women. When I had just that right level of buzz, that looseness, I was ready for any woman.

I often wondered what the women did before they hit the clubs. Bet they had a way to warm up too. And just before I sobered up, I asked a woman I met in the Copacabana on St. Catherine Street what she did. And do you know what she said? Well, she told me about a white wine routine she did with her girl friends at her place. They usually drank those cheap, two liter bottles of Niagara white wine. Smart. Started at home. Talked about how "

The studs of the world could serve them best. Saved time. Skipped the tavern step. And when she finally got to the bar or disco, she'd nurse one drink all night or wait until a guy bought her one after a couple of slow dances. Took about one and three-quarter slow dances to know if it would happen. She could tell by his body movements on the dance floor if he had any stamina, which was paramount to her. Do you come often? she asked me.

It was always the same."

Counting Cars

"Most nights my father would tell me to keep a sharp eye out the living room window. This was after I asked when Mom would be home. He would tell me to keep counting cars and, when I reached at least one hundred, my mother would walk in the door. We lived on a side street and there was never much traffic. On rainy nights, each car could be heard and was easier to count. Many times I would be counting way past my usual bedtime. My father tried to be nice by offering me bribes, or being strict by threatening to tell my mother how I waited up for her, anything to get me to bed. Finally, he gave up and let me sleep on the living room floor. He knew. He knew I would not leave the front window until I knew my mother was home safe, until I heard her singing and mumbling into an invisible microphone in her fist as she staggered up our sidewalk. Usually, by that time, I ran out of numbers.

A week ago I asked my dad why my mother behaved like she did. He told me to go to my room, get on my knees and thank God for not making me like her. And that night, I slept as if my heart were being flung back and forth from the North Pole to the South Pole.

But you know, on her good days, my mother sang like a professional and used our salt shaker for a microphone and I swear she sounded better than the song on the radio."

First Time

"After I told another person about my resentments, fears and sex problems, I went for a long walk to a huge quarry with my dog. Used to come to this enormous hole in the ground to get drunk alone and play with the idea of plunging into that dark hole so I could stop feeling the fear. However, I suddenly noticed how perfectly blue the sky was and how perfectly white the ice-cream clouds were. The orange and yellow and blue chests of some birds stood out like tiny flags from friendly foreign countries. Even the water in the quarry was clear and my reflection looked right through me. My dog sat beside me and, for the first time ever, without prompting, offered a paw, like a boy in a dog-suit. When I peered down into the water, I saw every single member of my family dressed in their Sunday best and lined up according to age. Each was waiting to shake my hand and tell me that my amends had been accepted. Everyone was filled with a grace so easy I could touch it in the air. Above me, the sun reached down, wrapped me in gold and held all my womanhood with a touch so light, you'd think I was being kept afloat by some kind of family breathing."

Fourteen Years

"Do I sound like Clint Eastwood yet?

Hey, I'm fourteen years sober today. That means another round of puberty. That means I'll start getting pimples on my face and then the scars. That means my voice will change. I may grow taller. Put on weight, muscle. Buy clothes to actually look good. That means I can start dating girls and maybe I can restart a relationship that doesn't revolve around only me. That means action down below. That means I'm heading to maturity and adulthood, even though my mirror tells me my hair is almost gone and my belly button birthday says I'm forty-nine years of age. I'll be fine, as long as I don't drink, just for today. I fantasize about having a twenty-five-year-old girlfriend. Does anyone know how old Clint's latest wife is? Bet Clint does.

Once I thought that the word 'maturity' was overused, and should be applied to an overripe prune or banana only. But, I figure I've been full of prunes all my life and I've been slipping on banana peels from the time I took my first steps. A boy my age worries about hair loss but I won't borrow one of Clint's hats so I'll remember that my recovery is an inside job."

Dry Spot

"My second husband was a good drinking buddy but that was it.

As our marriage went on, we drank ourselves out of our socks and it got worse and worse. Reached a point that when we went to parties, my husband would hide some of the host's own booze somewhere in the house just to be sure we had enough to drink at the end of the party.

Finally, I had to stop and joined Don't Drink. I made some new friends and got my hands on that Don't Drink book. I was told to take it home, leave it on my coffee table and read its pages. That second husband of mine got really jealous after awhile, as if the book were some guy I was seeing on the side. And one night he came home so drunk, smelling like a convention of skunks. Shouting like he was being attacked, my husband flung my Don't Drink book right out the living room window. It was pouring rain and I was furious but I was also very afraid. After letting him have his usual rough, drunken, horny sex with me, I fell off that narrow shelf of fear into sleep.

Next morning, he got up and left for work before I did. I could still smell the stale stink of last night's booze and cigarettes and I nearly lost my stomach in the bathroom sink. I could hear my head throbbing. See my temples move in the mirror. Then, I threw on my coat and went outside to find my special D.D. book. There it was on the road, still looking good, in the middle of the dry spot where my husband's car had been parked."

Till My Eyes Watered

"My mother had an alcohol phobia because her own father drank himself inside out. Each night, when my dad watched a baseball game, he'd ask one of the four of us kids to go fetch him his one can of beer from the fridge. That was all my mother allowed him to drink. A few cold sips was all he ever wanted to drink anyway. Whenever it was my turn to get him his beer, I'd rush to the fridge and nearly rip off the fridge door. Then I'd tear open the tab and drink from the can until my eyes watered. My father didn't mind or notice. I was about seven or eight when I started drinking from his one can of beer. My brother and two sisters would watch and watch, counting how many seconds it would take for my eyes to water up. Then, they'd try to tug the can from my grip and bring it to my father but never succeeded. Meanwhile, my father just smiled and waited patiently for the two or three gulps that were left. My watered-up eyes were a harmless joke to him. He knew the less beer he drank, the happier my mother would be.

It took awhile but my mother gradually became afraid of me."

Perfume And Socks

"My mother drank so much that I smelled whiskey on her all the time. In addition, she forced us to take off not only our shoes when we came home, but also our socks so we wouldn't get lint on the carpet. If she looked mean when we arrived home, we knew she was really drunk and we yanked off our shoes and socks faster than we could close the front door. We also knew there was big trouble whenever Mom stapled the living room curtains to the wall because she was afraid someone outside might be watching her drink. Other girls at school talked about the perfume their mothers wore and occasionally would have some dabbed behind their ears and on their wrists. So one day, I dipped my finger into a glass that had some whiskey left at the bottom and dabbed lots of it behind my ears. I dabbed and I dabbed until I smelled exactly like my mother. When I went to school, my friends said I smelled funny and I told them it was my mother's real perfume. That's all I ever smelled on her and I honestly thought it was just her own perfume. Well, we all lined up in the hallway and took turns sniffing one another's fragrances. The teacher noticed. The Principal noticed. My mother received a phone call from the Principal. When I got home, my shoes and socks were taken off before I even opened the front door because I saw my mother at the front window.

Have you ever begged the sun to stay high in the sky?"

Table of Contents